SHOUT

A PLAY BY
MEL DONALSON

This book is dedicated to my family members who have given me much inspiration, support, frustration, and joy. They have collectively contributed to the many ways in which I perceive and respond to the major jubilations and the minor earthquakes in life. Much love to Wilbert, Dorothy, Beverly, Paulette, Brian, Derek, John Jenkins, Pete, Wilfred Samuels, Fred Lamster, Gini & Tim, Justin & Elida, Jill, Reggie, James, Harold & Elaine, Joe & Delores, Marcus, Lily Ruth, Michael Whitted, Desmond, Naomi, D'Andrew, Corinthia, Bridgette, and Lee

CHARACTERS

AMELIA ROSEWALL…White, 22-years-old, with a sensitivity hidden beneath a surface bitterness. Jeffrey's daughter.

JEFFREY ROSEWALL….White, 50s, with an assertive manner and creative temperament.

QUINCY TURNER….Black, 50s, articulate and quick-witted. Jeffrey's best friend.

MAGGIE AUSTIN….White, mid-30s, smart and good-hearted to a fault.

SIERRA TURNER….Latina, 50s, thoughtful but direct. Quincy's wife.

SIMONE FORCHE….White, 40s, independent, and self-contained.

KEN MURA….Japanese American, 20s, opinionated, educated, but not wise.

SETTING

Manhattan….Spring 1997

The PLAYING STAGE can be arranged into six separate environments with a combination of set construction, props, and area lighting:

Jeffrey's Townhouse – Interior, located upstage. This is the widest, fixed construction. This area will suggest a kitchen at upstage right and a living room at upstage center.

Jeffrey's Townhouse – Balcony, exterior, located downstage left. This area is emphasized with area lighting.

Jeffrey's Townhouse – Exterior, Street, located downstage center. This area is emphasized with area lighting.

The Theater – located downstage right. This area will be suggested with a small table with three chairs and shown with area lighting.

Penn Station – located at downstage center. This area will have a bench and shown with area lighting.

Quincy's Home Office – located at downstage left. This area will be suggested with a small table with a phone and shown with area lighting.

ACT ONE

Scene One

(The lights come up slightly, but the stage remains dim. A screen is lowered as a Cello solo plays a poignant melody entitled "Amelia." Numerous slides appear, showing an attractive white woman in her 30s. This is CHRISTINE. In a montage of images, she is playing the Cello, typing at a computer, reading a book, holding a baby proudly, drinking a glass of wine, smoking a cigarette, and then laying in a hospital bed. The final two images show a headstone and a formal head shot of Christine smiling. As the last image fades, the screen rises.

A spotlight hits downstage center, and AMELIA ENTERS and takes her mark. She's dressed casually and holds a green journal. She begins reading a poem, but after a few lines, she recites by heart.)

AMELIA: Looking for salvation outside myself,
arms opened hopefully for someone else,
in this quicksilver moment of loneliness
and living at the margins I must confess
the many ways we need each other,
a comforting sister, a caring brother,
self respect—the armor protecting my sanity
self love—the gravity securing my humanity

don't suffocate me with your sameness,
whirling me into a void of some aimless
pursuit for me to be what you choose to believe,
all I ask, in peace, is to let me breathe,

no sanctuary of solace in your rigid demands,
I sing my solo voice, and here I stand

(The spotlight goes dim, as AMELIA EXITS.)

Scene Two: The Theater

*(The lights come up downstage right on the Theater.
QUINCY and JEFFREY ENTER from the wings.
JEFFREY holds a clipboard with notes. They linger at a
table with two chairs. There's a briefcase on the table,
and one of the chairs holds a woman's jacket and
purse.)*

QUINCY: You know...since you made those
blocking changes, the last act takes on
a surreal tone. I like it.

JEFRREY: You don't think it's too contrived? Having
the jury move from the box to down stage.

QUINCY: No, it plays well. But your first idea was even
better...having the jury actually go into
the audience and sit. Letting the audience
become the jury. Symbolic, but effective.

JEFFREY: Yeah? Tell that to our producer. He refused
to give up six first-row seats for the jury
to sit in. According to him, bad business...we
would lose seventy-five dollars a seat.

QUINCY: Mmm, yet another painful example of art
bending to commerce! Is there no end to
this sacrilege?

JEFFREY: The producer's worse than those Japanese
we dealt with.

QUINCY: As I remember, we weren't going to bring up
that project again. Water under the bridge, right?

JEFFREY: It's more like sewage.

QUINCY: Remember our mantra—Sugihara! Sugihara!

JEFFREY: Yeah, yeah! I'll keep my promise and not
talk about it. I'll just keep my anger focused on
that idiot of a producer.

QUINCY: You know, he does have a name.

JEFFREY: Yes, but if I say his name three times,
he'll cross over from the underworld and
stay on our side.

QUINCY: Ah, yes, I think I saw that movie…and the
sequel.

JEFFREY: As I remember, you were in that movie…and
the sequel.

QUINCY: The things I do for my craft. In our acting
workshops, they neglected to warn us about
the part of the business we would regret.

JEFFREY: Believe me, it wasn't funny when the
producer and I argued about it. I came close to
killing that little pencil-neck budget king!

QUINCY: And, no doubt, there's a pencil dick to go
along with that pencil neck! You should've
produced the play yourself.

JEFFREY: No, I needed to focus on the writing and
directing. This play means too much!

QUINCY: Well, you've done a wonderful tribute to
Christine. Her poetry never sounded better.
Hearing her words, she's truly alive again.

JEFFREY: Yes. She was a remarkable talent! I often
wish things had been different.

QUINCY: It's a wish wasted, my friend. You both had to
follow your own hearts. There was too much
that pushed you two apart.

JEFFREY: More like running in separate directions...
but always connected through Amelia. Q,
you think I failed her as a father? Maybe Amelia
would have been better off with Christine?

QUINCY: We'll never know, my friend. When I think of
Brandon, I wonder if Sierra and I told him
too much. Didn't tell him enough. Didn't demand
enough! Parenting is a guilt-ridden experience.
Imagine the sleepless nights Adam and Eve had
after Cain killed Abel. Did Eve breastfeed Cain
long enough? Did Adam play catch with him?
Was it that damn snake's fault again? In those
days, they couldn't blame Cain's behavior on the
media or rap music! So, you know they were up
late at night blaming themselves. But...it doesn't
do any good. All you can do...is all you can do!

JEFFREY: Yeah...guess you're right.

> *(ENTERING from the wings, MAGGIE breaks into their conversation as she puts on her coat. The three conduct a bantering which they have obviously enjoyed many times before.)*

MAGGIE: Aren't you two done yet? I'm hungry!

QUINCY: You're always hungry. Jeffrey, part of your duty as director of this play, not to mention being the designated lover of the leading lady in this play, is to make certain that she's well-fed.

JEFFREY: Yes, but by being the director, I'm accountable to Mildred in wardrobe who will flog my hairy butt if the leading lady gains an ounce before this production is over. It's my obligation to keep Maggie as luscious and sexy as she is!

> *(JEFFREY and MAGGIE kiss briefly.)*

MAGGIE: I'm still hungry!

QUINCY: *(theatrically)* No food should pass those lips where a kiss of love has sweetened the tip of the tongue and the edges of the nose, the fingers, the knees, and the toes!

MAGGIE: I'm still hungry!

QUINCY: Well, Jeffrey, I tried. Good poetry usually fills an empty stomach.

MAGGIE: Yes, *good* poetry does!

JEFFREY: (*looking at clipboard*) Speaking of good poetry, I need to give Allen a couple more notes before he leaves. (*to MAGGIE*) Just give me a sec.

(*JEFFREY EXITS off stage right*)

QUINCY: So, how're you two doing? Despite my pleadings, it seems like love.

MAGGIE: I'm afraid so. At first, I thought…just a quick scratch of a sexual itch. What people in New England call Puritan love.

QUINCY: Puritan love?

MAGGIE: Yeah, you know—very quiet, very functional, very quick! But I've never been so…intoxicated by someone! You know the actor's oath—get the role first, to hell with anything else!

QUINCY: And now?

(*MAGGIE sits and leans forward thoughtfully.*)

MAGGIE: I still want the career. But I can't see it meaning anything if Jeff's not there. There's this wonderful and unexpected way he's become…necessary. I can't really explain it.

QUINCY: Well, you two have something in common, then. He feels the same about you.

MAGGIE: That took me by surprise even more.
Particularly considering his past...the stream of
leading ladies.

QUINCY: Stream? More like the ocean at high tide.

MAGGIE: Okay, I get it. But that's who Jeffrey *was*.
Much of that had to do with Christine.

QUINCY: Then, you know that Jeffrey's a good man.
And if he said he loves you, it's the truth.

MAGGIE: Thanks, Q. It all scares me a bit. Trusting.
Sometimes, it's hard to get beyond my
past...the years I was bounced around...one
foster home to the next...fighting off drunken
husbands until I couldn't fight anymore.

QUINCY: It takes miracles and a lot of luck to survive
a broken system.

MAGGIE: System? The system had a name...hell!
I've used amnesia to cope. I do remember being
sixteen when I met this cute boy. He stole a car,
and I ran away with him. We got out of North
Carolina and made it to... (*making dramatic air
quotes*) New York City! I woke up one winter
morning in this construction site we slept in, and
he and the car were gone...along with what little
money I had. A waitress at a coffee shop took
pity on me. I slept on her couch for months. She
later died of a stroke...I made it to the Village...
waitressing and acting classes. One day I was
lucky enough to tell a convincing lie that got me
my first show.

QUINCY: Well, my dear, you've certainly earned your
      career.

MAGGIE: That's one of my concerns. I've always taken
      care of myself...now I'm thinking marriage.
      Living *with* and *for* someone else! Hopefully,
      we can have something as special as you and
      Sierra.

QUINCY: Yes, we have a special kind of marriage. She
      loves me deeply, and so do I.

      (*QUINCY sits at the table.*)

MAGGIE: You're impossible.

QUINCY: Yes, most nights. Here's the thing. When I
      met Sierra, I had landed a part on a cop show.
      We were shooting these scenes in the Bronx,
      and the fans were watching it all. Afterwards,
      I went over to the crowd. Saw Sierra...this
      beautiful woman, and time stopped! I asked her:
      "you want my autograph?" She said without
      hesitation: "No, I want you to donate to our
      community center!" She put a flyer in my
      hand with the info and walked over to the next
      actor. *(chuckling)* Took me a month to track
      her down. But that month led to twenty-eight
      years of joy, and arguments, and more joy!

MAGGIE: That's beautiful.

QUINCY: So is she. Sierra has this mountain of a

personality—generous to a fault. Yet, she cuts
through any nonsense and finds the truth! She's
my Bronx Baby! *¡Mi corazón!

MAGGIE: So, want to share some marriage secrets?

QUINCY: Secrets? Well, in all of these years, I've never
allowed Sierra to see me naked.

MAGGIE: (*chuckling*) To keep the mystery?

QUINCY: No, I don't want to overwhelm the poor
woman.

MAGGIE: No, really. I'm frightened to death about
taking that step.

QUINCY: Well, it all comes down to what you're
looking for in the union with another person.

MAGGIE: What were you looking for?

QUINCY: Freedom.

MAGGIE: You got married to be free? I don't follow.

QUINCY: (*seriously*) For me, marriage is not about
being tied down. It's about being released. To
have the freedom to be yourself at anytime!
Most people enter marriage holding on so tightly
to expectations and limitations, they smother the
union before it can develop. They use fairy tales
and clichés to build cages, and then wonder why
the marriage doesn't soar.

MAGGIE: Interesting philosophy. I'll let it marinade a bit in my thoughts.

QUINCY: (*lighter tone*) A wise choice. I was never one for accepting new ideas like some sushi bar. Stir fried, grilled—yes! But never accept new ideas in their raw form. It's healthier that way!

MAGGIE: I'll remember that. But, I'm still dealing with this fear.

QUINCY: That's a good sign.

MAGGIE: You think so?

QUINCY: It means you're using your head *and* your heart to balance off all of that wild sex you two have been having. (*as they both laugh*) Oh, here comes the stud now.

(*JEFFREY ENTERS. Joins them on stage.*)

JEFFREY: Well, Q, we've got to be going. Maggie's ready to take her bite of the big apple. I've seen that cannibalistic look before. It's a seven-course gaze, with a twinkle of pasta in her eyes.

(*QUINCY stands.*)

QUINCY: Well, the eyes have it then. And I must be off myself!

MAGGIE: Remember, Q, tomorrow evening. You and Sierra are joining us. Dinner's at seven.

QUINCY: We'll be there with a Merlot in hand?

MAGGIE: No, I was scolded by the Oenophile at my
market for picking up a bottle of Merlot.

JEFFREY: The what?

QUINCY: Oenophile. A fancy word for wine snob.

MAGGIE: Well, he said that a Merlot is too pedestrian
and classless.

QUINCY: Oh, really? Well, if he's a wine snob in his
heart, it means he has sour grapes in his soul.
I read that in the mid-80s, there was a Chateau
LaFite Bordeaux that sold for more than
$100,000. But I would prefer a $10 bottle of
Merlot any day.

MAGGIE: And why's that?

QUINCY: Merlot is a wine for revealing secrets.

JEFFREY: Oh, not this story. It's been a long day.

MAGGIE: No. Go ahead. I want to hear it.

QUINCY: Well, the story goes back to Twelfth
Century legends, to Merlin the wizard.

MAGGIE: As in King Arthur? The fictional character.

QUINCY: My dear Maggie, there's always the factual in
fiction. Always the truth behind the lies. Secrets
behind the silences.

MAGGIE: Go on.

JEFFREY: Don't encourage him, Maggie.

QUINCY: Disregarding the constant interruption,
      here's the story. As you know, Merlin was
      deeply in love with the Lady of the Lake. In his
      love, he revealed to her all of his secrets, all of
      the keys to his magical wisdom.

MAGGIE: Then, she placed a curse on him and locked
      him away in a tower or something.

QUINCY: Not exactly, but you're close.

JEFFREY: (*to Q*) I'd like to lock you away.

    (*QUINCY places a cautionary finger to his lips
    to silence JEFFREY.*)

QUINCY: Now, the Lady of the Lake was known by
      many names. Truth is, being from the land of
      Avalo, she had been named Bella D'Avelo.
      Bella is Latin for beautiful. And, indeed, Bella's
      beauty captured Merlin's heart. Their love
      spanned lifetimes, but was as brief as a day. You
      see, they both became consumed with jealousy.
      He of her superior gifts for learning his wisdom
      so quickly. She of his endless gifts that were still
      to be taught.

MAGGIE: So, they were jealous over the same thing.
      The gifts. The talents.

QUINCY: Yes, and they both understood this truth.

Jealousy would ruin their love. So, using all of their magical powers, they spun this sin of jealousy from their spirits and locked it into a whirlwind of sounds. They shouted out this horrific affliction that was consuming them both and buried it into the soil of the dark Celtic earth. It was their secret. No one would ever know.

MAGGIE: So, what happened?

QUINCY: Well, the rains. The spring rains drenched the Celtic soil and carried their buried secret into the neighboring vineyard. A vineyard then bore a harvest of dark, hard grapes. The grapes carried the essence of their jealousy, but also carried the sounds of both their names. The first part of his name—*Mer*, and the last part of her name—*lo*. And the story goes that if you drink the Merlot, you will confess the secrets within.

MAGGIE: And if I drink the wine without confessing? What happens?

JEFRREY: You get drunk! Like Q and I have done on many occasions.

QUINCY: Are you sure you want to marry this man? This unbeliever!

(*MAGGIE steps over and places her arm around JEFFREY's waist.*)

MAGGIE: Yes, I do! And don't let him fool you. He's a believer.

QUINCY: Well, I believe that you believe that he
　　　　believes. So, Merlot it is. Until then...ciao, my
　　　　children of the night!

　　　　*(QUINCY EXITS. JEFFREY and MAGGIE hug
　　　　again. But JEFFREY's mood suddenly turns
　　　　serious as he gathers his briefcase and jacket.)*

MAGGIE: What's wrong? It can't be the play. I've never
　　　　seen a cast as ready as this one. Never seen such
　　　　splendid directing!

JEFFREY: No, it's not the play.

MAGGIE: Then, it's Amelia.

　　　　*(JEFFREY packs his clipboard inside before
　　　　putting on his jacket.)*

JEFFREY: I've looked forward to tomorrow night for a
　　　　long time. Now, that it's here, I'm not so certain
　　　　I'm ready for it. But, it's time Amelia deals with
　　　　the truth, and she may see it all as rather ugly.

MAGGIE: The truth can only be what it is. Neither ugly
　　　　or pretty. You've told me that Amelia's been
　　　　angry at you for years.

JEFFREY: Her anger has morphed into madness.

MAGGIE: I know you've been a terrific father!

JEFFREY: Well, I never imagined that raising Amelia

would bring such...a feeling of futility. It's like an earthquake that never stops. I'm always trying to find my balance!

(MAGGIE steps to him. Gives a comforting touch.)

MAGGIE: I can't begin to understand what you're going through! (*apprehensively*) Do you think she'll *like* me?

JEFFREY: In a New York heartbeat!

MAGGIE: But, if she doesn't?

JEFFREY: Then we'll suffer the little vampire for a week and send her packing back to the caves of Ithaca. But, you've laid the groundwork. The cards you've sent her...the phone calls.

MAGGIE: But, she never responded to the cards...the phone calls were like monologues on my part.

JEFFREY: Well, she's a busy college senior...exams, classes, drunken orgies.

MAGGIE: Have you told her we're talking marriage?

JEFFREY: Not yet. I wanted to wait until she gets here. I'll tell her after she and I have discussed the situation about her mother.

MAGGIE: You're right. Jump one canyon at a time.

JEFFREY: Amelia's really a beautiful girl underneath. She'll love you. My fear is that after tomorrow night, she may not love her mother anymore.

(The lights go down.)

Scene Three: Penn Station

(The lights come up at mid-stage. The SOUNDS suggest the interior of the busy train station. At center stage, there's a bench. AMELIA ROSEWALL and KEN MURA ENTER from stage right. She carries a small overnight bag, while he labors with two large suitcases. Although we only see AMELIA and KEN throughout the scene, we hear the noisy chatter, the footsteps, the whistles, the ANNOUNCER's VOICE calling out destinations.

At center stage, AMELIA abruptly stops. She turns to KEN who's preoccupied with balancing the luggage.)

AMELIA: I don't want to do this!

KEN: What?

AMELIA: I don't want to see him!

(KEN eyes the free bench nearby.)

KEN: Over here.

(They move to the bench. KEN is obviously relieved to be sitting. AMELIA searches her overnight bag and pulls out her StarTAC Flip Phone.)

AMELIA: I'll call and say I'm sick…can't make it.

KEN: Cricket, no! We've discussed this ad infinitum. We'll stay for three days and then back to Ithaca to spend the rest of the vacation together.

(AMELIA nods and puts the phone away.)

AMELIA: It's going to be difficult enough dealing with *him*. But, there's this Maggie person.

KEN: Well, you've managed to put off meeting her for months. Maybe, it's time to see her face to face.

AMELIA: God, she's been sending me these cutesy cards…like I'm some patient in a nursing home.

KEN: I'm sure she's just trying to open up things between the two of you.

AMELIA: Things! What things? She's living with my *him*. The man who fooled around on my mother. The man who's twenty years older than her. She's just another aspiring actress who thinks that opening her legs is the best way to open on Broadway!

KEN: If she were that shallow, I'm certain your father wouldn't be with her. After all, he's been in his profession for what? Thirty years or so? Don't

you think he would know the users and the
losers?

AMELIA: My father's a walking cliché. A sexual
vampire biting victim after victim...preferably
blonde and early 30s.

KEN: That's a poetic image. But you said he raised you
by himself *and* still earned his share of fame.

AMELIA: Believe me, there were quite a few nannies,
housekeepers, and boarding schools along the
way. He raised me so he could shut my mother
out! It was *his* choice. I never had a choice.

*(KEN reaches out and places his arm around
her. In the background, the NOISES continue.)*

ANNOUNCER'S VOICE: First call! The six o'clock
express for points south! Now boarding on
platform twelve!

KEN: Hey, I'm here with you. And I'm looking forward
to meeting your father. But if the tension gets to
be too much, just give me the word, and we're
out of there!

(They kiss briefly.)

How're you feeling now, Cricket?

AMELIA: Better. Thank God Aunt Simone will be
there.

KEN: That's your mother's sister?

AMELIA: Yes. She's absolutely the best!

KEN: The fashion editor, right? I'm just trying to get the players straight before the game begins.

AMELIA: Put her at the top of your list. Since mother's death, she's the only one I've talk to...except for you, of course.

KEN: So, what kind of woman is she? Living in the fashion universe, is she anorexic, addicted, catatonic?

AMELIA: She's wonderful! Creative, but a savvy business woman...travels all the time! She's gorgeous...extremely feminine...always stylishly dressed!

KEN: So, you get your looks from your mother's side of the family.

AMELIA: You wait until you meet her. At one time, I thought of following her lead...being on that planet of designers, fashion shows, catwalks, globe-trotting with the trendsetters!

KEN: But, instead you write poems...like your mother.

AMELIA: And I'll be a college professor.

KEN: Like your mother. And?

AMELIA: And?

KEN: And to play the cello.

AMELIA: (*sadly*)Yeah, like my mom.(*excitedly*) There's this game that Aunt Simone and I play. Our own version of black jack. We call it twenty-one quotes. It's how she got me to read in junior high. At any point in a conversation, she would say "quote," and then she'd recite a line from a book on our reading list. Then, at the end, she would say "unquote," and I had to guess the author and the book. If I was right, I'd get one point.

KEN: (*understanding*) And you kept going until you got to twenty-one.

AMELIA: Right. And I could do the same to her. It would take us months to play out one game. But, the first one to twenty-one would be treated to an ice cream sundae.

KEN: Cute. But suppose you guessed right, but she lied.

AMELIA: Aunt Simone and I would never lie to each other.

KEN: So, who kept score?

AMELIA: Well, we've sort of kept a running score.

KEN: Mm-hmm. I have a feeling you were treated to a lot of ice cream sundaes in junior high.

AMELIA: Yep, but I've read a lot of books, too.

KEN: Well, my grandparents were always my dealers

for my ice cream addiction. What about your grandparents?

AMELIA: I never knew them. No grandparents on either side.

KEN: Oh...(*lifting the mood*) So, let's see...there's your mother—the poet, scholar, musician. Your father's a successful writer-director. Your aunt's the fashion designer.

AMELIA: Oh, there's also Uncle Q and *Titi*.

KEN: Who?

AMELIA: Quincy Turner and his wife, Sierra.

KEN: Quincy Turner—the actor?

AMELIA: Yes. And *Titi* is a well-known painter.

KEN: I don't know if I'll fit into such an impressive family.

AMELIA: You'll be the lawyer in the family. And the man I love!

KEN: But I'm a long way from making the kind of money your father does.

AMELIA: If you become rich—great! But if we live one paycheck at a time, I'll still love you and be there for you!

KEN: Will you, really?

AMELIA: Of course. I'm crazy about you!

KEN: How crazy?

AMELIA: Crazy enough to break out into one of those
silly love songs like they did in the old movie
musicals!

KEN: That's not crazy, that's scary! You can't sing!

AMELIA: Then, I'm crazy enough to...(*standing*) to
shout out to the world that I love you! I'll do it
right here!

KEN: (*playfully*) Hey, settle down, you wild woman
from Ithaca!

(She takes his hand and the two embrace.)

AMELIA: Is that crazy enough for you?

KEN: Are all poets as mad as you?

AMELIA: It's not madness. It's passion!

*(They kiss affectionately, forgetting they're in a
public place. The ANNOUNCER's VOICE
brings them back to where they are.)*

ANNOUNCER'S VOICE: Second and final call for the
six o'clock southern express. Stopping at
Washington, D.C., Baltimore, and Lynchburg.

KEN: (*matter-of-factly*) I have family in Lynchburg.

(*devilishly*) You know, the hardest part about this visit will be sleeping without you for a few nights. You know how I love to reach over and grab a handful.

(*He rubs the outside of her thigh.*)

AMELIA: Well, being a nun is not what I planned for spring break.

KEN: You hate *being* a nun! I hate not getting none! (*with intended sexiness*) Maybe, there's an elevator at your dad's place. We can sneak away and hide inside. Push the buttons so it goes up and down, as we go up and down! And what's it called when you slide your fingers up and down on the cello?

AMELIA: Glissando. Ken, you're nasty!

KEN: Maybe they have elevators here?

AMELIA: You're cute when you're horny.

KEN: Then, I'm cute most of the time.

(*They kiss briefly.*)

AMELIA: Let's get a cab. What's-her-name's making dinner.

KEN: Remember to compliment her on the meal.

AMELIA: (*sarcastically*) I promise I'll say what I'm feeling!

KEN: That's what frightens me!

(She takes a deep breath.)

AMELIA: Okay, let's do this before I turn around.

(KEN lifts the suitcases.)

KEN: Take me home, beautiful!

(They EXIT. The lights go dim.)

Scene Four: Jeffrey's Townhouse--Interior

(The lights come up in the interior of Jeffrey's fashionable and comfortable home. The Living Room is in the center, displaying tasteful decorations. Displayed prominently of the wall is a FRAMED PAINTING—a work by Sierra Turner. Contemporary furniture is visible, including a couch, end tables, a coffee table, and two chairs. A PHONE is centered on one of the end tables.

At stage right is the Kitchen Area, partitioned off, where a table with three chairs is visible. The cabinets, countertops, sink, and refrigerator can be suggested.

In the Kitchen area, MAGGIE places foil around the edges of a casserole dish.)

MAGGIE: *(calling loudly)* Jeffrey, are you finished yet?

(JEFFREY ENTERS from the wings, stage right. He carries a wine glass, rubbing it clean with a dish towel.)

JEFFREY: (*Gesturing to off stage right*) The dining table's set. Plates and silverware at attention. And there're enough flowers to give the dining room that jungle décor you seem to be going for.

MAGGIE: Well, you said Amelia likes flowers. And this dinner is doubling as a birthday celebration for her.

(JEFFREY places the dish towel and glass on the table. He goes to her and places his hands on her shoulders.)

JEFFREY: You've knocked yourself out! I want you to know I appreciate all you've done!

MAGGIE: I know. Everything's ready. I'll put the casserole in the oven when everyone gets here. (*checking watch*) It's six-thirty. You told Amelia to be here by seven?

JEFFREY: She wouldn't let me meet her at the station. But she would've phoned if there was a delay.

(Overlapping JEFFREY's speech, the intercom buzzes. JEFFREY leads MAGGIE to the living room and the intercom near the door. He presses the intercom button.)

Yes, Nick...Right, send her up.

MAGGIE: Is it Amelia?

JEFFREY: Yes. Show time…first act. I hope I don't
forget my lines.

MAGGIE: Don't worry. You know how to improvise.

JEFFREY: I love you.

(*They share a brief kiss.*)

MAGGIE: Should I give you two a few minutes alone?

JEFFREY: No, you stay right here with me.

*(The doorbell chimes, and JEFFREY opens the
door to AMELIA and KEN. There's a strained
pause as JEFFREY and AMELIA seem
uncertain as to how to greet one another.
Finally, JEFFREY reaches out for a hug, but
AMELIA offers her cheek for a light kiss. KEN
smiles generously as he ENTERS, glad to be
resting the suitcases. KEN reaches out and
shakes JEFFREY's hand.)*

KEN: I'm Ken Mura. A pleasure to meet you, sir!

*(KEN extends his hand. JEFFREY, baffled,
reaches out to shake hands.)*

JEFFREY: Hello…Ken. And Ken, this is Maggie.

*(MAGGIE moves forward. Shakes KEN's hand.
Then, she quickly embraces AMELIA. No
response. AMELIA walks into the interior as if*

*MAGGIE were invisible. So, MAGGIE steps
back to JEFFREY, and there's an awkward
moment as the four stand in silence.)*

KEN: Great to meet both of you at last! And thanks
for inviting me!

*(JEFFREY and MAGGIE exchange confused
glances. Then, simultaneously, JEFFREY,
MAGGIE, and KEN all take a long look at
AMELIA. She has smartly managed to distance
herself from the three.)*

AMELIA: Ken, I just didn't feel like explaining
who you are over the phone.

KEN: Well, Mr. Rosewall, I hope I'm not intruding.

JEFFREY: Not at all. Maggie's got Amelia set up in the
guest room, and, Ken, the couch is a convertible.

KEN: That'll be fine.

AMELIA: *(defiantly)* No! Ken will sleep with me in the
guest room. I'm twenty-two now, and, more
importantly...Ken and I are engaged!

*(There's another awkward silence. KEN sighs
out loud as he steps between AMELIA and
JEFFREY.)*

KEN: Mr. Rosewall, we were going to tell you tonight…
(*looking at Amelia*) at dinner!

JEFFREY: Amelia prefers it this way, Ken. Surprise…
shock! A good old-fashioned kick in the nuts!

*(The air is thicker with tension as JEFFREY and
AMELIA stare at one another.)*

MAGGIE: Ken, the guest room is down the hallway on
the left…and, then, I'll give you a tour.

*(MAGGIE and KEN EXIT stage left into the
hallway leading to the bedrooms. AMELIA
walks deeper into the Living Room. JEFFREY
closes the front door and walks to her.)*

JEFFREY: Look, Amelia. Let's use this visit to talk…to
listen. Obviously, I need to get to know this Ken
person. You need to know who Maggie is.

AMELIA: He's not just some person. He's my fiancé!

JEFFREY: If you insist.

AMELIA: And I already know *what* she is! Something
young and moist to get you through this phase of
your career!

JEFFREY: Stop right there! Regardless of your feelings
against me, Maggie has done nothing to you!
See her for who she is.

AMELIA: I've seen her before! Different name,
    different face, but the same package! And I've
    heard all of this before!

JEFFREY: No, Amelia, you haven't heard *all* of it.

AMELIA: Let's be clear as to why I'm here. You
    have a birthday present that my mother left for
    me. You insisted that I get it in person. As far as
    I'm concerned, you can give me the present
    now, and Ken and I will leave!

JEFFREY: Why didn't you tell me about the
    engagement? I have a right to know!

AMELIA: No, not really. When it comes to me, you
    have no rights. Oh, yes, the court gave you legal
    custody, but that's all you've ever had.

JEFFREY: Amelia, you and me...we're all the family
    that we have.

AMELIA: No, Aunt Simone is family, too! And
    now, Ken.

    *(JEFFREY takes out a pack of cigarettes. He
    removes a cigarette, but doesn't light it.)*

JEFFREY: (*lifting cigarette*) Maggie helped me to
    stop smoking at New Year's. But I still like
    holding onto one.

AMELIA: And I wanted to hold onto my mother!

JEFFREY: Amelia, we discussed this at her funeral.

AMELIA: Discussed? As in, I sat while you insisted
you did what was best for me.

JEFFREY: Your mother and I decided together. And it
was her desire that you come with me.

AMELIA: Please, spare the lies! Mom's dead, and
you have the audacity to pile your lies on her
grave. *You* took me away from her, and I'll
never forgive you for that!

*(The two stare at one another. At that moment,
MAGGIE leads KEN back into the Living
Room.)*

MAGGIE: *(to Ken)* And the master bedroom is down the
other end of the hallway. It has a balcony with a
marvelous view.

KEN: Hey, Cricket, how about a walk on the balcony?

AMELIA: Yes, why not. The view from here is rather
old and nauseating.

*(AMELIA crosses quickly, and she and KEN
EXIT into the wings. JEFFFREY sits heavily,
and MAGGIE walks behind the chair where
JEFFREY sits. She rubs his shoulders gently.)*

JEFFREY: In less than five minutes, my child has
insulted us both, opened old wounds, and
cut some new scars. Quite a gift she has.

MAGGIE: I didn't realize she was so...spiteful! Did
you know about Ken?

JEFFREY: Well, when we spoke at Thanksgiving, she mentioned she was dating someone. But I had no idea she was this serious. God, engaged!

MAGGIE: They're so young.

JEFFREY: Young and confused. And he's what? Chinese? Korean? What's "Mura"?

MAGGIE: Sounds Spanish. Anyway, I guess we'll have to ask him. Is that a problem?

JEFFREY: What? Him having a Spanish name?

MAGGIE: No...the fact that he's Asian.

JEFFREY: It's just...unexpected. I had prepared myself for that day when she'd float in here with some boy on her arm. But not tonight! And certainly I didn't expect some immigrant to be at her side!

MAGGIE: Why do you assume he's not American? Even if he's not, what of it? Don't let her spoil our evening!

JEFFREY: All I'm saying is, who is he? What does his family think of Amelia? I'm certainly not orthodox, but Yom Kippur and Hanukkah mean a great deal to me. God, a Jewish princess marries a Kung Fu Master! Sounds like one of those awful cable movies!

MAGGIE: That's a little harsh, isn't it?

JEFFREY: I'm not...(*takes a breath*) listen, let's not talk about this now. I already have a headache from my joyous reunion with my daughter. My neurotic daughter!

MAGGIE: And who's responsible for that?

JEFFREY: Yes, yes, I know...Maybe, Christine and I made the wrong decisions for Amelia.

MAGGIE: It'll be all right. You two will have time to talk through everything by the end of the week.

JEFFREY: Yeah, a long day's journey into a nightmare. I just hope I can make it through this evening.

(The intercom buzzes again.)

MAGGIE: That must be Simone.

JEFFREY: Oh, God, here comes round two.

(MAGGIE crosses to the intercom. Pushes the button.)

MAGGIE: (*into intercom*) Yes, Nick...that's right. Show her in.

(MAGGIE goes to the door. Opens it. Seconds later, SIMONE FORCHE ENTERS. SIMONE is confident and professional in a stylish business suit. She simmers with sexuality—her voice, her walk. She carries a bottle of wine and offers a cordial smile.)

MAGGIE: Simone? Hi, I'm Maggie. We've been
voices over the phone. Glad we're finally
meeting!

SIMONE: Maggie, hello.

> *(The two women shake hands. SIMONE passes
> over the bottle of wine.)*

Merlot, right?

MAGGIE: Exactly. Love your outfit. Is that stretch knit?

SIMONE: No, it's not domestic. It's an imported wool
crepe. Warm, comfortable...a slight touch of
exoticism.

JEFFREY: Like you? Hello, Simone.

> *(As SIMONE steps deeper into the Living Room,
> MAGGIE closes the door. JEFFREY stands to
> greet SIMONE. They shake hands briefly.)*

SIMONE: Hello, Jeffrey.

JEFFREY: You're still looking fit.

SIMONE: I spend enough time at that damn health
club. I'm glad the long workouts are paying off.
Amelia here yet?

JEFFREY: Out on the balcony...with somebody
named Ken.

SIMONE: So he did come...good.

JEFFREY: You knew about this guy?

SIMONE: Amelia and I talk every week. But I don't detect any unbounded joy coming from the father of the soon-to-be bride.

MAGGIE: He's still in shock. (*to Simone*) A glass of wine?

SIMONE: Love one.

> (*MAGGIE EXITS into the Kitchen. JEFFREY offers SIMONE a chair. They sit in silence for several seconds.*)

JEFFREY: I meant what I said. Time has been kind to you.

SIMONE: You seem surprised.

JEFFREY: No, no, I don't mean it like that. I know how difficult it's been for you.

SIMONE: At least you have Maggie.

JEFFREY: Yes, she's made the difference. Still, I do want to thank you for keeping your ties with Amelia. She adores you.

SIMONE: And I love her. She's Christine's daughter.

JEFFREY: Yes...are you sure you want to go through with this?

SIMONE: Are you sure?

JEFFREY: It's the way Christine wanted it. By the way, Quincy and Sierra will be joining us.

SIMONE: That's fine by me. (*a beat*) I read about your play. How's the production going?

JEFFREY: (*knocking on wood*) Very good. Previews next week.

SIMONE: I'm sure you did Christine well.

JEFFREY: Well, her courage inspired the story. And she wrote such hypnotic poetry. Will you be coming to opening night?

SIMONE: No. After tonight, I'll probably never see you again.

JEFFREY: I understand.

(*The lights go down on the Living Room.*)

Scene Five:
Jeffrey's Townhouse Building—Exterior

(*The lights come up downstage. The SOUNDS of vehicle engines and horns pepper the air.*

From stage right, QUINCY and SIERRA TURNER ENTER. They walk slowly as SIERRA leans the right side of her body on the walking cane held firmly in her right hand. QUINCY carries a decorative bag containing a bottle of wine. SIERRA stops and touches QUINCY's arm.)

SIERRA: Q, wait just a moment.

QUINCY: Something wrong? If you don't feel up
      to this, we can turn around for home.

SIERRA: No, they're family, and I want to do
      whatever I can to help.

QUINCY: So, what is it?

SIERRA: It's this weekend…

QUINCY: I know. His birthday.

SIERRA: There's less pain in the memories now.
      The hurt has broken into smaller fragments over
      the years. It doesn't weigh as heavily on my
      chest anymore. But…I can still see the
      sweetness in his face. Can still hear that devilish
      laughter.

(QUINCY adjusts her shawl as he speaks.)

QUINCY: For me, I still get this glimpse of him
      walking…that Brandon walk! All confidence
      and energy…mixed with just enough arrogance.

SIERRA: Like his father.

QUINCY: Well, he had to get *something* from me. He
      got his intelligence and good looks from you!

SIERRA: Listen, smooth talk like that doesn't
        guarantee that you'll have your way with me
        tonight.

QUINCY: That's why I placed the bottle of
        amaretto on the bed stand. Two glasses of that,
        and you'll just cave in to my charms.

SIERRA: After two glasses, I'm all caved in, period.
        I won't be able to see a thing you're doing.

(He kisses her affectionately.)

QUINCY: Well, when you wake up, that man next
        to you in bed with a big smile on his face, that'll
        be me. So, are you ready to do this?

SIERRA: Okay, but…it's going to take more than wine
        and your quick wit to get me through this
        gathering.

QUINCY: Not to worry. I know where Jeffrey hides the
        hard liquor!

(The lights go down.)

Scene Six:
Jeffrey's Townhouse—The Living Room

*(MAGGIE returns with glasses of wine for SIMONE and
JEFFREY. She hands them out.)*

MAGGIE: Let me go and check on the lovebirds.

(MAGGIE EXITS downstage left into the wings.)

SIMONE: I hope I don't make you feel uncomfortable.

JEFFREY: No. And I'm sure this is awkward for
you. But for Amelia's sake, I think we can be
civil to one another tonight.

SIMONE: Agreed. And if it means anything under
the circumstances, I think you've been a good
father.

JEFFREY: Thank you for that.

*(Suddenly, AMELIA's voice calls out as she
ENTERS.)*

AMELIA: Aunt Simone!

*(SIMONE, places her wine on the table, rises,
and goes downstage to meet AMELIA.)*

SIMONE: Amelia, darling!

(The two women hug.)

AMELIA: I can't tell you how good it is to see you!

SIMONE: Same here. And a belated happy birthday!
Look at you! Twenty-two! Intelligent, beautiful!

AMELIA: Not half as much as you! Thanks for the
gift you sent. The outfit stands out in my
wardrobe of jeans and t-shirts! So, where are
you flying off to next?

SIMONE: To Paris again. Tomorrow night.

AMELIA: No! That only gives us a short while to visit! (*smiling suddenly*) Quote: "They didn't welcome death, but were too weary to live their lives of desperation and pain. A world of darkness and deceit." ...unquote.

(SIMONE steps back and touches her chin thoughtfully. JEFFREY remains anchored silently to his chair.)

SIMONE: Mmm...Virginia Woolf? *Mrs. Dalloway*?

AMELIA: Nope! Gertrude Stein...*The Desperate Women.*

SIMONE: Point yours. So, where do we stand now?

AMELIA: I believe I'm leading by a few points. *(steps closer again)* I have much too much to tell you!

JEFFREY: I'll give you two time alone.

(As JEFFREY rises, the intercom buzzes. He goes quickly to answer it.)

JEFFREY: *(into intercom)* Yes...right. Thank you. *(to the women)* It's Q and Sierra.

(JEFFREY steps back towards AMELIA and SIMONE as if he is about to speak. But he doesn't, and the three stand silently. An uncomfortable pause. AMELIA turns her back to

JEFFREY as she touches SIMONE's hand.
SIMONE responds with a smile.)

With her wine in hand, SIMONE follows
AMELIA's tugging lead downstage right, as they
ad-lib a secret discussion.)

JEFFREY: (*sarcastically*) I'll just get the door.

(JEFFREY opens the door, and, ENTERING,
QUINCY guides SIERRA inside. JEFFREY hugs
her and then closes the door after QUINCY.)

SIERRA: Jeffrey, you're scowling!

JEFFREY: This is my survival expression.

SIERRA: So, Amelia's here.

JEFFREY: Mm-hmm, in full force!

QUINCY: Before we go any further, here's my
favorite Merlot. Are we still revealing secrets
tonight, or did you change your mind?

JEFFREY: The way things are starting, we're going
to need a case of wine.

SIERRA: (*chuckling*) I warned him.

JEFFREY: You're right as usual, Sierra! But I'll
gladly take the bottle you have. Maggie's
planned a different wine for each course tonight.
It's all been planned down to the final crumb of
the crumb cake.

(JEFFREY closes the door.)

QUINCY: Sierra and I will brace ourselves for the gourmet event.

SIERRA: Oh, hush, Q. Being here saves me from spending another evening at home with your stories.

QUINCY: *(to Sierra)* I'm crushed by your honesty. Couldn't you just lie for my sake?

JEFFREY: It's good to see *you*, Sierra.

SIERRA: And you, too. *(calling out)* Simone, hello, it's been a long time.

> *(SIMONE turns from her conversation with Amelia and meets SIERRA half way. They embrace.)*

SIMONE: Hello, Sierra! And Q! Last time I saw you two....

QUINCY: Two years ago...at Christine's funeral. *(stepping towards Amelia)* And you, young lady, come here.

> *(QUINCY and AMELIA hug one another.)*

AMELIA: Hello, Uncle Q.

QUINCY: Hello, and I'm late in wishing you a happy birthday!

AMELIA: Thank you. *(to Sierra)* Titi!

SIERRA: *¡Mi cariño!* It's been too long.

QUINCY: (*to Jeffrey*) And Maggie? Is she in the kitchen phoning for take out?

JEFFREY: She's out on the balcony.

QUINCY: Jumping to avoid eating her cooking?

JEFFREY: I won't tell her you said that. Come on in the kitchen with me, and I'll get you a glass.

> *(QUINCY touches SIERRA's shoulder before he and JEFFREY EXIT. AMELIA guides SIERRA's careful steps into the Living Room. The three women sit.)*

SIERRA: (*to Amelia*) So, catch me up with all the news in your life. Have you heard from any grad schools yet?

SIMONE: I was just about to ask that myself.

AMELIA: (*to Sierra*) Aunt Simone knows the good news already—I'm engaged!

SIERRA: *¡Dios mio!* That *is* indeed…news! When did this happen?

AMELIA: Ken proposed on my birthday.

> *(AMELIA proudly lifts her hand and shows the engagement ring.)*

SIMONE: (*to Sierra*) She made me promise not to tell
anyone.

SIERRA: (*glancing at the ring*) It's lovely, Amelia!
But I'm upset that you didn't call me!

AMELIA: I wanted to, but Ken's a bit old school,
and he wanted to have a big announcement
at dinner! That man-in-charge bullshit!

SIMONE: I know it well.

AMELIA: But, I insisted that Aunt Simone know!

SIERRA: But, Amelia, you'll soon be graduating. And
you're planning on going on for a doctorate. Are
you really prepared to commit to a marriage?
Have you thought it through?

AMELIA: (*excitedly*) I didn't have to think long. Ken
knows I plan to get my degree. Besides, he's
going to law school, and he understands that
graduate school is going to be a part of our
marriage to begin with. When you meet him,
you'll see. He doesn't chase women like most
men. He's committed and faithful...plus he's
smart, funny...handsome!

(At that moment, KEN and MAGGIE ENTER.)

KEN: *(interrupting)* Did you mention the part about
me being handsome?

*(AMELIA stands and escorts KEN over to
SIMONE.)*

AMELIA: Aunt Simone, *Titi*...this is Ken Mura!

KEN: *(shaking hands.)* A pleasure to finally meet
you both! *(to Simone)* Cricket talks about you
constantly...*(to Sierra)* and I understand you're
an artist.

AMELIA: *(pointing to the framed art)* This is one
of her paintings...a gift to Mom when she
became ill.

KEN: *(looking closely)* Wait, I've seen this painting
before. *(recalling excitedly)* My freshman
year with my study group...a weekend trip
here to the city...the exhibition at the
Whitney Museum...you're *that* Sierra?

SIERRA: Only if you enjoyed the paintings.

KEN: Oh, absolutely. And I remember this one because
it's uncomplicated, but alluring. A cello merges
with a heart. They become one-in-the same, but
the heart is broken...joy and sorrow bound
together. Am I right?

SIERRA: If that's what you see and feel, then you're
right.

KEN: It's captivating. And I remember your work
because *you* only signed a one-name moniker.
So, what's your full name?

SIERRA: Sierra Clemente y Zaragoza de Turner.

KEN: Oh. Well, I thought your work was really

bold—like Frida Kahlo.

SIERRA: I'm sure that's a compliment, but Frida
was Mexican. I'm Puerto Rican. And my
pathway to this moment was quite different than
hers.

KEN: Oh, I'm sorry...didn't mean to suggest anything.

SIERRA: *(smiling)* That's okay. One of my students
thought I was Carmen Herrera...she's Cuban
and in her early eighties.

AMELIA: *Titi* teaches art classes at the University of
Stamford.

KEN: I see. So how long have you been in America?

SIERRA: Well, I've been a citizen all my life. But
after finishing at the School of Visual Arts in
San Juan, I studied here at the New York
Academy of the Arts. Does that help?

KEN: No, I didn't mean... *(gesturing at painting)* So,
what's the title?

SIERRA: *"Christine."*

AMELIA: *(emotionally)* It was Mom's favorite piece.

KEN: I can see why.

SIMONE: *(a lighter tone)* So, please sit, Ken. Sierra
and I have a few questions for you.

(They all move to claim a seat)

KEN: I expected as much. Okay, ladies, fire away!

(The lights down in the Living Room.)

Scene Seven: The Kitchen

(The lights come up in the Kitchen where JEFFREY busies himself with pouring wine for him and QUINCY. JEFFREY drinks quickly and pours another.)

JEFFREY: Why am I putting myself through this hell, Q?

QUINCY: Because you love your daughter. But getting drunk won't make it easier.

JEFFREY: Can't hurt. Anything I say to her brings on another emotional explosion.

QUINCY: Emotions are tricky, my friend. When Sierra and I had Brandon at home, dramas came in tidal waves. But like Brandon, Amelia's worth fighting for.

JEFFREY: Yes…but then, she brings this kid home.

QUINCY: What kid?

JEFFREY: Her fiancé I've been told.

QUINCY: What? Are you joking?

JEFFREY: If only I were. I enjoy eating in the tatami room at Miyasaki's Restaurant, but not at home.

QUINCY: Jeffrey, you're babbling. This is just another storm to weather.

JEFFREY: No, this time it's a tsunami!

(JEFFREY sits heavily at the table across from QUINCY.)

QUINCY: Between you and Simone, you'll work it out.

JEFFREY: God, the wicked witch of the catwalk!

QUINCY: I know, but you need her tonight. So, do you know anything about Amelia's fiancé?

(JEFFREY empties his glass quickly and then pours another.)

JEFFREY: He could be Japanese, Korean, Chinese. Take your pick.

QUINCY: Oh, I see. *(sarcastically)* He's one of *those* people.

JEFFREY: Oh, please, Q. Don't you start!

QUINCY: Don't start? Am I supposed to sit here and listen to you drop your venom? That's the way it always starts! Little drops, and then the racism is airborne.

JEFFREY: (*angrily*) Don't go stepping onto that
pedestal. I've dealt with these people! I don't
need it in my home!

QUINCY: Are you talking about the young man
with Amelia, or the investors who walked out on
our deal? (*angrily*) God, Jeff, I thought we were
all done with that. Yeah, that whole project went
down the sewer! But that's because they were
terrible businessmen, not because they were
Japanese!

JEFFREY: Oh, come on! I worked my tail off on that
deal! I lost $200-grand!

> *(JEFFREY can't contain himself. He stands and
> moves in agitation.*

QUINCY: It wasn't just your ass on the line! It was my
name used to package the deal...remember?

JEFFREY: And you were just as pissed off and ready to
murder them as I was! So, don't give me that
"let's-rise-above-it" bullshit!

QUINCY: No, don't rise above it. Forget it! Let it go!
I have! And don't resurrect that dreadful deal
through Amelia's fiancé. Give the boy a chance!

JEFFREY: Don't get sanctimonious with me! I've
heard you say your share of comments about
white people.

QUINCY: Yes, you have. And I plead guilty for

generalizing. But, right now, I'm talking about you and your daughter, and the man she wants to marry. You're dismissing this kid before you've had a chance to know him. And I'm saying that's wrong!

JEFFREY: Wrong! Why? Because I won't see my daughter involved with someone who's not right for her!

QUINCY: (*rising, the table between them*) Not Right! A quick glimpse of his complexion and facial traits! Is that all it takes?

JEFFREY: Spare me the toleration speech! I don't need this shit from you tonight!

QUINCY: What you need is a good kick in the ass!

JEFFREY: You're twisting this into something ugly!

QUINCY: It *is* ugly! We've both dealt with our share of this poison. How many times did the cops stop me when I left your building? How many of your neighbors called the cops before they took the time to talk to me?

JEFFREY: That's why I'm concerned. I know what's waiting for her with this boy!

QUINCY: Hopefully, she might beat the odds, and at the very least, she deserves that chance.

JEFFREY: I don't remember you being happy when
Brandon was dating that white girl... Shania?
Shelby? Whatever her name was!

(QUINCY sits again, chuckling slightly)

QUINCY: That's because she drank too much. The
girl had a problem. She was eighteen, and she
was in my house only a few hours before
emptying the bar.

JEFFREY: Oh, the white girl your son dated
conveniently had a problem. It had nothing
to do with her being white!

QUINCY: Come on, Jeff. Just before Brandon died, he
was in love with...some other white girl.

JEFFREY: *(taking a breath)* Really? You never told me.

QUINCY: No, I didn't. But here's my point. Brandon
went to Dartmouth, in the snow drifts of New
Hampshire. I would've been surprised if he
hadn't been involved with a white girl. But, I tell
you something...if I could have Brandon with
me here and now, I wouldn't care if he was
dating a three-eyed, toothless, one-legged alien.
(a beat) Jeff, Amelia came home with someone
she cares about. No matter how terrible it may
all seem...don't lose this time with her!

(The lights in the kitchen go down.)

Scene Eight: The Living Room

(The lights come up in the Living Room.)

SIERRA: So, Ken, your last name is pronounced
        Moo-rah?

KEN: Well, it's spelled M-U-R-A, but I pronounce it
     mirror...like the looking glass.

MAGGIE: Well, you all get acquainted. I'm back to
        the kitchen.

SIMONE: *(to Maggie).* Jeffrey's in there with Q.

MAGGIE: Mm, I thought I heard their voices. And
        thanks for the warning.

        *(MAGGIE EXITS. SIMONE and AMELIA sit on
        the couch. SIERRA sits in an easy chair at stage
        left. KEN sits in the chair at stage right that puts
        his back to the kitchen.)*

SIERRA: So, Ken, are you at Ithaca College, too?

KEN: No, Cornell.

SIMONE: And I hear your plans include law school?

KEN: That's right. Harvard in the fall.

SIERRA: Impressive! Have you spent time in the
        Boston area?

KEN: Yeah, Cambridge and Boston are ideal...small, full of history...and seafood restaurants!

SIMONE: Are you from the New England area?

KEN: No, Southern California...Orange County. A small city called Irvine...an hour south of LA.

SIERRA: So, how did you find your way to upstate New York for college?

KEN: I always wanted to see the real America. The northeast has so much history and tradition. In southern California, history is defined by whatever happened last week.

SIMONE: Do you miss the west coast?

KEN: Not really. But I do miss my family. I have a big family with uncles and cousins who take up several blocks of homes along the same street.

SIMONE: It must be great to have a large family. I wasn't so lucky.

KEN: It's made a big difference in my life.

SIERRA: So, how many brothers and sisters?

KEN: Three brothers, no sisters. But there're enough girl cousins to keep Maybelline into profits.

AMELIA: Ken's going into criminal law.

SIERRA: Really? Not corporate or business law? That's where most young people are headed these days.

KEN: No, not me. After watching *the* trial, I made up my mind!

SIMONE: *The* trial?

> *(QUINCY ENTERS with two glasses of wine. KEN doesn't know QUINCY is behind him.)*

KEN: Yeah, the trial where a certain black athlete got away with double murder. They should've had the trial in my old neighborhood. *My* jury would've put his black ass away with all the rest of his kind!

SIERRA: *¿Que? ¡Eso es una cosa terrible de decir!* Exactly, what do you mean? *Ay Bendito!*

KEN: Oh, no! I wasn't suggesting—

> *(KEN sees AMELIA gesturing. SIMONE smiles. SIERRA shakes her head. KEN looks over his shoulder. KEN stands up quickly.)*

KEN: My God! You're Quincy Turner!

QUINCY: That's right. Black ass and all. Here, take a glass!

> *(Ken takes the glass. Quincy offers a glass to Amelia)*

AMELIA: None for me, Uncle Q. I'm not drinking.

KEN: This is unreal! Quincy Turner! Cricket said
you would be here. You're my father's favorite
actor! And here you are serving me a drink!

QUINCY: No, no, I'm not serving you. *But*, if that's
the way you want to tell the story in the old
neighborhood, feel free to.

KEN: No, what I mean is, this is really an honor.
And I apologize for what I said. I was just
rambling on.

QUINCY: As you're doing now. Please, sit down,
young man, and tell us more about your legal
theories.

KEN: (*to the women*) Can either one of you rescue me?
I'm feeling a bit of an idiot right now.

*(AMELIA gets up and stands next to KEN. She
touches him proudly.)*

AMELIA: (*to Quincy*) This is Ken Mura—the man I'm
crazy about!

SIERRA: Q, it seems these two are engaged!

QUINCY: So I've heard. Congratulations!

KEN: I'm really the lucky one in the deal. Cricket is
unique!

(AMELIA gushes and gives KEN a quick kiss.)

QUINCY: And how did you and...*Cricket* meet?

KEN: At Cornell. I was leaving my College
Republicans' meeting, and stopped off at the
undergrad library to get out of the cold.

AMELIA: And I was on his campus for a poetry
reading. And I stopped in the library to get out
of the snow.

QUINCY: So, fate and the elements brought you
together.

AMELIA: I guess you could say that.

QUINCY: (*to Ken*) So, Cornell...an Ivy League
man. How do you like the university?

KEN: It's great! The standards they set there are
extremely high! I was real fortunate to get in.

QUINCY: Yeah, Cornell's had a memorable
political history.

KEN: For sure. I was a member of the College
Republicans' student caucus last summer to the
national convention in San Diego. We strongly
pushed for the Pro-Life Amendment to be in the
platform. Dole and Kemp should've won!

QUINCY: Well, the political action I'm referring to
was the 1969 armed takeover of a campus
building by the black students at Cornell.

KEN: Oh, yeah. I remember hearing something about it.

AMELIA: Ken's not telling you about his "A"
    average for the last three years. He's brilliant!

QUINCY: Must be to have that kind of achievement. My
    nephew applied to Cornell, but didn't go.

KEN: Was it his grades? Cornell does have a good
    Affirmative Action program.

QUINCY: No, his grades were fine. He decided to
    go to my alma mater instead.

SIERRA: (*to Ken*) It's good you chose law and not
    public relations.

KEN: I'm sorry. I didn't mean anything. When I'm
    nervous, I tend to talk too much!

QUINCY: As you're doing now.

KEN: Sorry. So, tell me, Mr. Turner, how did you
    first meet Mr. Rosewall?

QUINCY: Let's see...

SIERRA: It was after you left Brown.

QUINCY: Yes, yes, that's right.

KEN: You went to Brown? You're Ivy League, too.
    How did you like Brown?

QUINCY: Intellectually stimulating. But, culturally
    and emotionally... let's just say that I was black
    and *blue* at Brown. But, I graduated and made

my way to New York. Jeffrey and I met in an acting class.

KEN: Sounds like a long friendship.

QUINCY: Jeffrey and I owe each other a great deal of money, so we keep in touch. Now, this pet name you have for Amelia—Cricket.

SIMONE: Yes, I'm a bit curious myself?

AMELIA: Don't you dare tell them!

KEN (*playfully ignoring Amelia*) Well, once Amelia and I started...seeing each other, it turns out that when she first gets into bed at night—

AMELIA: (*interrupting*) —That's because it's always cold at your place!

KEN: As I was saying, when she gets into bed, her feet are ice! So, she has this habit of rubbing her feet together as she makes this high-pitched sound, and...well, you have to be there!

QUINCY: Oh, I get the picture clearly. You've just reduced the woman you love to an insect. Rather Kafka-esque, but who I am to judge young love!

AMELIA: Since we're telling secrets, everyone should know that I call Ken "Boo-Bear"! You remember when I was a kid, Uncle Q, when you bought me my Boo-Bear?

QUINCY: It was a signature moment in my life.

SIERRA: So, Cricket and Boo-Bear are going to marry.

QUINCY: Your honeymoon is certain to be an
episode on *Wild Animal Kingdom!*

> *(MAGGIE and JEFFREY ENTER. JEFFREY
> carries the dish towel, and MAGGIE removes an
> apron.)*

MAGGIE: Is everyone ready?

SIMONE: Yes, good timing. Quincy was just beginning
his life story.

QUINCY: (*with mock pain*) Et tu, Simone? And I was
beginning to enjoy your company!

JEFFREY: Well, Maggie has prepared some marvelous
dishes.

MAGGIE: Actually, it's a special meal for our special
daughter.

AMELIA: (*emphatically*) I'm *not* your daughter!

> *(The air immediately becomes heavy.)*

MAGGIE: Oh, of course not, Amelia. I wasn't
implying anything. I just wanted—

AMELIA: (*interrupting*)—Oh, I know what you
want! You want *him* and all the money and
attention that comes with it!

JEFFREY: That's enough, Amelia! It's one thing to

target me, but I—

AMELIA: (*interrupting*) —To target you! You make
    it sound like you're the victim here! For once,
    would you face up to the truth?

SIMONE: Amelia, please don't do this!

AMELIA: No, Aunt Simone, for years I've had to
    accept the way he wanted things. He divorced
    Mom, and got custody of me! He put me in
    boarding schools! Then, he sent me away to
    college! (*to Maggie*) And now you... another
    young starlet for his trophy case!

MAGGIE: (*calmly*) I'll go and put the bread on the
    table.

AMELIA: No, Maggie, don't go! You should know
    how you fit into his story line. My father
    structures life like he does his scripts! Always
    controlling...manipulating!

SIMONE: Amelia, we need to sit and talk calmly.

AMELIA: No, I think Maggie needs to know that
    she's not the first. Has he told you about all the
    others, Maggie? How his affairs ran Mom away?

KEN: Hey, Cricket, we're a bit tired. Let's eat first...
    try to have a pleasant evening.

AMELIA: Pleasant! *(to Jeffrey)* It hasn't been pleasant
    since the day I walked in from school and found
    you picking up your bimbo's panties and bra!

JEFFREY: Stop it, Amelia. You were twelve-years-old. You couldn't understand!

AMELIA: I understood that you were here with another woman! God, I even heard her singing in the shower! And so I ran out of here, and got as far away as I could! (*to Jeffrey*) Are you going to deny it?

JEFFREY: I'm not denying anything tonight.

AMELIA: So, why not tell Maggie! Who was it? Some student from a writing class? Some actress in heat? Just who was it?

SIMONE: It was me!

> (*Silence. SIMONE's words pierce the air, floating like a dark cloud. SIMONE moves closer to AMELIA.*)

AMELIA: What?

SIMONE: It was me, Amelia. I was in the shower.

> (*AMELIA shakes her head, staggers.*)

AMELIA: It can't be! It can't be! Mom said she was with you.

SIMONE: Yes, she was.

> (*The lights fade to black.*)

-END OF ACT ONE-

ACT TWO

Scene One: The Living Room

(The stage is dark. A cello solo reaches out through the darkness—a haunting melody filling the air. The lights come up on the interior of the Townhouse. In the Living Room, QUINCY, SIERRA, and MAGGIE sit patiently. KEN, agitated, paces as he glances towards the kitchen. QUINCY and SIERRA nurse their glasses of wine, while MAGGIE handles a cigarette she never lights.)

KEN: *(to all)* You think Amelia's okay? You think I should go in there?

MAGGIE: No, let them talk.

QUINCY: Should've been done long ago.

SIERRA: Too many questions left unanswered.

KEN: Why didn't Mr. Rosewall tell her?

MAGGIE: This is the way her mother wanted it.

QUINCY: She was afraid for Amelia. I think it's understandable.

KEN: But this is 1997, not the nineteenth century.

QUINCY: Yes, but surely you would agree that even in 1997, in certain old neighborhoods, the jury would be rather unforgiving of Christine and Simone's relationship.

(KEN walks over to QUINCY.)

KEN: Listen, Mr. Turner, I meant no disrespect by my
my earlier comments. The reality is that a certain
criminal element in our society has a certain
racial identity.

QUINCY: I would suggest that there are many
criminal elements in society. Some criminals of
certain racial identities are constantly paraded
before viewers on the six o'clock news. Then,
criminals of another certain racial identity are
constantly organizing the parades.

KEN: But look at you. You're a black man who's
done well. I learned that it's all about busting
your butt to get what you want! Like you...
you've made an impressive career! You're not
one of them!

QUINCY: One of them? I assume you mean that as a
compliment. The flip side being that I must be
one of you.

SIERRA: Ken, you're attempting to defend an
indefensible position. I would hope that you
were a more...analytical thinker.

KEN: Well, I think being rational is the key! Listen,
my parents were Japanese immigrants, and
they made it. It wasn't easy for them to break
through the barriers. But they did! They paved a
way for me and my brothers to all go to college!
No handouts! No excuses! You're a decent
person, Mrs. Turner...and you, Mr. Turner.

You've both worked hard to reach your goals!
You're wealthy... famous. And with hard work,
anyone can attain their dreams. That's what our
society's all about!

QUINCY: Ah, meritocracy! Yes, ideally, that's what
our society's all about. But remember, there's
the ideal and then there's the real.

KEN: And we have to always aim for the ideal.

QUINCY: True, but we have to live the real.

KEN: Maggie, you see what I'm saying, don't you?

MAGGIE: I'm afraid my views would be a bit too
cynical. Compared to me, Q is a sunny optimist.

KEN: Oh, God, I'm stranded in a sea of liberals and not
a drop of common sense to drink.

QUINCY (*thoughtfully*) Common sense. Well, indulge
me, Ken, and allow me to tell you a story...about
Boo-Bear.

KEN: What do you mean?

SIERRA: Oh, Q, not that story again. Can we at least
have the short version?

KEN: Is this a story about the ideal or the real?

QUINCY: A bit of both. You see, when Amelia was,
maybe four...like most kids, she feared the dark.
Her nightmare? A big black bear hiding in the

closet. Jeffrey and Christine began reading her
stories about Winnie the Pooh, trying to assuage
her fear. And, sure enough, the image of Winnie
slowly erased that frightening vision of the big
black bear. But at her age, she couldn't say Pooh
bear, so it came out Boo-Bear! Well, I wanted to
do my part in helping her to break through her
fears. So, one day after a workshop, I took
Amelia down to a department store to buy her a
toy bear. After searching, we found one that she
liked, and as we neared the cashier, two white
uniformed security men approached me, one on
either side. They identified me as a thief who
had plagued the store before and rushed me off
to a room, isolating Amelia in another room.

KEN: That's illegal! You hadn't attempted to leave
the store with any merchandise.

QUINCY: They were white. They had guns. They had
suspicions. It was legal for them because I was
black! For an hour, they detained me until two
city police officers arrived who were also white.
One insisted that the security guards were
correct. That I matched a description of, as you
call it, a criminal element of a certain racial
identity. They tried to force a confession out of
me by using language that they, no doubt,
picked up during their police training. Then, in
addition to being accused a thief, they wanted to
know why I was with a little white girl. Who
was she? Where were her parents? Back-and-
forth, on-and-on...but having neither the
intelligence nor the vocabulary to mince words

with me, they finally gave up their tactics of
interrogation.

KEN: Good.

QUINCY: Not really. Frustrated that they couldn't
get a confession of guilt, one officer pulled out
his gun and placed it three inches from my right
eye. It was no longer about stealing. It was no
longer about being with a little white girl. I, a
black man, had humiliated him and his
comrades. I had been impudent, confident, and
worse of all... innocent of their accusations!

KEN: So, what did you do?

QUINCY: It was the four of them against me. I
couldn't physically overpower them! They had
guns...badges! There were no witnesses, no
videotape! What would you have done?

(The lights quickly dim in the Living Room)

Scene Two: The Kitchen

(The lights quickly come up.)

*(JEFFREY, facing the audience, sits at one end of the
table. SIMONE and AMELIA sit on either side of the
table. On top of the table, there's a small cardboard box
and a container of tissues. AMELIA dabs at her eyes
with a tissue. JEFFREY pours more wine in their three
glasses. AMELIA pushes her wine glass far out of reach.*

SIMONE sips her wine and stands, leaning onto the back of her chair.)

SIMONE: What would you have done, Amelia? I
        loved Christine when we first met at Ithaca.
        After college, she came here to the city to do her
        grad work at Columbia. She was twenty-one,
        fearless, determined! I followed her here,
        stumbled into a job as a Buyer at Saks, and we
        lived together for a year. Then, Christine's
        parents came on a surprise visit. We told them
        the truth, and they turned their backs on
        Christine. So did her older sister and brother.

AMELIA: My grandparents are living? I have an aunt
        and uncle?

JEFFREY: Yes, you do.

SIMONE: You did. *(beat)* Christine expected their
        surprise, but she believed they would eventually
        respect the feelings we had! She was told to
        make a choice. And she gave up her family for
        me...for us!

AMELIA: But she could have—

JEFFREY: *(interrupting)* —let her finish, dear!

SIMONE *(sipping wine)* It was easier for me, I had
        been adopted, and what little family I had was
        already gone. Christine *was* my family, my
        friend, my lover...but, eventually, she needed to
        be on her own. We lost touch for a while, but a

few years later, I saw her...and we started up again, but by then...

(SIMONE finishes the glass. Reaches for the bottle.)

JEFFREY: By then, your mother and I were married, and you were just a baby. It was a busy time... with you, my first play produced and first screenplay sold all at once. And for years, I focused on work and more work! In and out of the city!

AMELIA: You knew nothing about them?

SIMONE: Not until he walked in that day and found us in the shower. He came back a day early from L.A....you were supposed to stay at a friend's. *(fighting back tears)* God, Amelia, I wanted to tell you. But your mother was afraid of how our relationship would affect you. And I was afraid of losing her, so I went along with it. For years, we masqueraded as sisters. And when the cancer took her, I wanted to scream out loud at her funeral! Just shout out all the secrets...all the love I had for her! All the life we shared together! But she didn't give me that privilege. She loved you too much to have people pointing and whispering and pitying and destroying! She loved you, Amelia! More than anyone else, she loved you!

AMELIA: But...what kind of love is built upon years of lying? It's all been lies hidden behind other lies. You call that love?

JEFFREY: Try to understand it from your mother's viewpoint. She had lost her family, her job...had lost Simone for a time. She wanted to spare you some of the misery that haunted her life. She hoped that when you became older, you would grasp it all...certainly better than you could as a child.

AMELIA: Well, guess what? Hearing this all at twenty-two is no better than facing it as a kid! You were wrong! Mom was wrong!

SIMONE: Was she, Amelia? She made the best decision that she could for you. The weight of all the whispering alone would have crushed you. She loved you and wanted to protect you. Tell me, what would you have done?

(The lights quickly dim in the Kitchen.)

Scene Three: The Living Room

(The lights come up quickly in the Living Room. QUINCY stands by the couch, moving back and forth as he speaks. KEN still stakes his position to easily watch the kitchen door. MAGGIE sits on the edge of her chair, while SIERRA watches KEN's nervous movements.)

QUINCY: So, I looked at the cop with the gun, filled my lungs with air, opened my mouth, and I shouted! Shouted until I was breathless! Until my chest ached!

KEN: Smart! That way someone would rush in.

QUINCY: No, I expected no help. No calvary. No
superhero in a cape. If the people standing
around the cashier didn't intercede when it first
happened, no one would be running into a closed
room. Seeing a black man being taken away by
white men in uniforms was just their sense of
what was normal. So, I shouted! Shouted
because it was my only weapon! *My* voice
bouncing from the walls and into their ears! I
understood that with a squeeze of the trigger that
man could end my life. But I knew that if he did,
my voice would continue to echo in all their ears
for all the nights to come. I would become *their*
nightmare monster in the dark! Well, maybe
they thought I was crazy. Maybe they realized
how insane the whole situation was. But, I stood
up slowly and walked out.

KEN: Did you sue?

QUINCY: At the time, I was a hungry actor. The two
lawyers I went to wanted retainers large enough
to buy me groceries me for a year. One civil
rights organization investigated, but there were
no prior complaints against any of the officers.
With no witnesses, the organization didn't give
my case any groundbreaking value.

(QUINCY sips his wine and sits on the couch.)

KEN: I can appreciate the trauma of that incident, but
those officers probably thought they were doing
their jobs. And maybe they went too far, but

maybe you shouldn't have verbally sparred with
them. In a way, you were controlling what was
happening!

SIERRA: I'm sure their efforts made the world a
safer place for all toy bears.

KEN: No, you're not hearing what I'm saying. You
have to see it from the other side, too. Maggie,
you see my point don't you?

MAGGIE: Your point is pointless, Ken. What
happened to Q was a disgrace!

KEN: I just see it differently, I guess. The officers
were merely protecting a child.

SIERRA: But Quincy told the officers the child's
name…her parents…the address and phone
numbers. We found out later that Amelia gave
them the same information. So, why did they
choose to disregard the facts?

KEN: That's a good point. But they had to be sure.

QUINCY: They were sure that I was black. That's
the one thing they were certain of.

KEN: It was unfortunate. But I just believe that
people live to do good. And in their efforts
at goodness, at the very least they reveal their
humanity. And in that human essence, some fall
short. That's where you find the racists.

QUINCY: But see, there's the mistake you're making.

KEN: What's that?

QUINCY: You're framing the situation in polarities. The
　　　　area in-between is quite real, and good people
　　　　can be racists.

　　　　　*(The silence suddenly ends the conversation.
　　　　　MAGGIE resumes her pacing, holding an unlit
　　　　　cigarette in the air. QUINCY fingers his wine
　　　　　glass. KEN eyes the Kitchen door as he walks
　　　　　near it.)*

KEN: God, what's going on in there?

QUINCY: A resurrection of Christine, I would
　　　　imagine. The question is whether Amelia
　　　　will believe in her mother or be a doubting
　　　　Thomasina.

KEN: *(to Maggie)* Aren't you going to smoke that
　　　　thing?

MAGGIE: *(lifting cigarette)* No, I can't. It's a
　　　　promise Jeffrey and I made to one another.

KEN: There sure have been a great many promises
　　　　made in this house. Mr. Rosewall and Amelia's
　　　　mother...Simone and Mr. Rosewall!

QUINCY: Don't be too quick to dismiss the value of
　　　　promises. Promises are the keepers of the best
　　　　part of who we are. Especially those promises
　　　　that come from the deepest chamber of the heart.
　　　　(a beat) Very much like the ones you and

Amelia will be making to one another on your
wedding day.

(KEN sighs and sits heavily in a chair.)

KEN: I guess you're right. *(lifting a glass of wine
from the table and sipping)* You know, it's
amazing! Simone! Who would've guessed it!
She's so...beautiful, feminine!

MAGGIE: You seem surprised.

QUINCY: What? She should look like Howard Stern
in drag?

KEN: No, of course not. But, you have to admit that
you were shocked when you first knew!

MAGGIE: Not really. In the theater...well, in the arts,
you'll find the whole spectrum.

KEN: I guess that *is* true of your profession.

QUINCY: And the legal profession! Including those
who sit on the bench!

KEN: Not that you'd know it.

SIERRA: So, are you upset that Simone is out in the
open or because she looks, as you say...
beautiful! Feminine!

KEN: You all are trying to make me into someone
evil. Bottom line is that I have no problem with
what someone is as long as he, *or she*, tows a

moral line of decency. Certainly, that's not too much to expect!

QUINCY: And how do you define this moral line? Certainly, the best of us are no better than the worst of us! If my wife were to go public with half the things I've said and done, *decency* wouldn't be the word to describe me.

SIERRA: Amen.

QUINCY: You don't have to agree so quickly!

MAGGIE: The same is true of my life. I'm like everyone else—a mix of virtue and vice! (*to Ken*) And what about your moral line of decency?

KEN: Well, I think of myself as someone who takes an honest and ethical approach to life. There's right, and there's certainly wrong!

QUINCY: Careful, Ken. You're trying to dance on quicksand.

KEN: What do you mean?

QUINCY: Earlier, you proudly told us about your parents...their sacrifices for you.

KEN: Yes, that's right.

QUINCY: And your parents were immigrants.

KEN: Yes.

QUINCY: And your name is Mura...Ken Mura. Are
   you being honest?

   (*KEN moves nervously and sips quickly.*)

KEN: Murayama...Keniko Murayama. I shortened the
   last name to Mura. You're twisting this. And I
   know where you're going. But it's not like that.
   I'm okay with being Japanese.

QUINCY: Then, why?

KEN: I wanted a name that's easier on the tongue.

QUINCY: Easier for whom?

   (*KEN throws up his hands in frustration.*)

KEN: Listen, the easier name avoids the stereotypes.

QUINCY: But in your zeal to escape the stereotypes,
   you become the very thing you seek to avoid.

KEN: No, I'm American.

QUINCY: But you lie about your family name. Are
   you saying that a person of color has to
   disappear culturally to become American?

KEN: No! I'm just saying that I'm not Hiroshima or
   Nagasaki.

QUINCY: But yet you are! You're also Sugihara.

KEN: Who the hell's Sugihara? Listen, I made a

choice that's honest to whom I see myself to be.
It's like the German philosopher, Kierkegaard,
once said...this isn't an exact quote, but...if we
lose honesty...suspend our ethics, we fall into
despair as a society!

QUINCY: Well, I'm not one for quoting dead white
men, but...if I'm not mistaken, Kierkegaard was
Danish. And what he suggested was that there
are those instances when a suspension of the
ethical avoids despair. So, he made a case for
what you did in changing your name. But he
also warned that such a choice is full of risks.
Left unchecked, it can eventually eat away at
one's soul.

KEN: (*sighing*) I've said it as simply as I can. An
honest and ethical life. Helping to create the
kind of society I want my child to be raised in.
There has to be acceptable behavior and
lifestyles! There has to be a dominating world
view that's right!

SIERRA: Well, Ken, I guess that depends upon who's
dominating!

(The lights go dim in the Living Room.)

Scene Four: The Kitchen

*(SIMONE, holding her glass of wine, paces. JEFFREY
stands, lifting Christine's green covered journals from a
cardboard box.*

AMELIA sits, sulking, a pile of used tissues forming a small mountain on the table.)

JEFFREY: As you know, I'm using your mother's poetry in my play. But Christine also kept journals. She began writing them when *she* was twenty-two...when her family disowned her.

SIMONE: Over the years, she wrote about all aspects of her life...and of course, you! Then, when she knew about her illness....

JEFFREY: Her desire, Amelia, was for you to know her. When you reached twenty-two, she wanted you to have her journals and her music.

SIMONE: I have her cello at my place...along with her music collections...Beethoven, Chopin, Debussy.

AMELIA: (*smiling slightly*) And the Bach suites...

SIMONE: Her favorites.

JEFFREY: She wanted you to have full ownership of her poems. Edit them...try to publish them if you choose. But no one else has ever read the journals.

AMELIA: (*sarcastically*) So...this is my legacy! Pages of shame and fear and secrets!

JEFFREY: No! Your legacy is your mother's courage. She dealt with rejection by her family...by society! She battled breast cancer for years! That's your legacy! Courage, creativity, and a lifetime of love!

AMELIA: And what am I supposed to do with these scribblings?

SIMONE: You can get to know your mother! You've attacked Jeffrey for years because you believed he kept you from her! Well, now you have the chance to know who she was!

AMELIA: Great! So I get to know that she was a closet case! What do I do with that, Simone?

JEFFREY: If you're half the woman Christine was at your age, you'll find your way to understand her!

(AMELIA rises. Places the journals back into the box.)

AMELIA: I don't want to hear anymore! Don't want to talk anymore!

(AMELIA takes the box and EXITS as the lights go down quickly.)

Scene Five: The Living Room

(AMELIA ENTERS as the lights come up. She proceeds briskly by everyone and EXITS off stage left and into the hallway to the Guest Room.)

KEN: Amelia! Are you all right?

> *(AMELIA doesn't answer. KEN follows her immediately.*
>
> *SIMONE ENTERS the Living Room. QUINCY, SIERRA, and MAGGIE watch her, waiting for the verdict.)*

SIMONE: Everything has been said, and Amelia's silence damns us all! (*to Maggie*)Well, sorry to ruin your dinner. You spent so much time preparing, and no one got a chance to eat.

MAGGIE: How're you doing?

SIMONE: It was as bad as I expected, but there's a sense of relief. To finally have it all out. But, there's an aching! I lost Christine, but I always thought that with Amelia in my life, a part of Christine would remain with me. But, now, I've lost Amelia!

> *(JEFFREY ENTERS. Moody. He carries a fresh bottle of wine. MAGGIE crosses to him. Gives a supportive hug.)*

JEFFREY: (*to Quincy*) Anything clever you can say my friend? I'm wordless at the moment.

QUINCY: Nothing clever. Just my admiration for what you've done as a father. And my respect for you, too, Simone!

> *(SIMONE walks to QUINCY. Extends her hand.)*

SIMONE: Thanks, Q. It was good to see you again.

(They shake hands.)

QUINCY: Take care.

(SIMONE steps to MAGGIE.)

SIMONE: Maggie, thank you for all you've done.

MAGGIE: Good bye.

(SIMONE goes to SIERRA and hugs her.)

SIERRA: Okay, my dear, be safe.

SIMONE: I will.

(JEFFREY moves for the Bedroom.)

JEFFREY: I'll get Amelia.

SIMONE: No, don't. If she ever cares to see me…she knows how to get in touch.

(JEFFREY nods. Places the wine bottle on the coffee table. He crosses to SIMONE, and they shake hands.)

JEFFREY: Maybe in time, Simone.

SIMONE: Perhaps…good-bye, Jeffrey.

(JEFFREY leads her to the door, and SIMONE EXITS.)

MAGGIE: Why do I feel so sad for her? (*to Jeffrey*) It
    you who's had to deal with Amelia's hatred all
    these years!

JEFFREY: Well…after Christine's funeral, Simone and
    I had a huge fight.

MAGGIE: How bad was it?

JEFFREY: Oh, God, enough swearing and name
    calling to repeal the first amendment.

SIERRA: Did it help?

JEFFREY: Don't know. Simone and I were both in
    love with the same person. And since we both
    lost her, the funeral was the last round. The last
    chance to punch away at all the frustrations and
    jealousies…the empty feeling of watching that
    coffin lowered.

    (*Jeffrey retrieves the wine bottle from the table.
    Lifts the bottle in the air.*)

JEFFREY (*to Sierra and Maggie*) Share?

SIERRA: Yes, please.

    (*JEFFREY pours a glass for everyone*)

QUINCY: A toast.

SIERRA: To Christine. * ¡Mi querida amiga!

ALL: To Christine.

(*They all raise their glasses in a salute. The lights dim.*)

Scene Six: The Balcony

(*The lights go up on AMELIA as she stands along looking out into the night. The SOUNDS of vehicle engines and horns drift up into the air. KEN ENTERS).*

KEN: Cricket, here you are!

AMELIA: God, I'm exhausted!

KEN: You must be.

AMELIA: (*sighing*) What a nightmare! I don't want to stay here any longer!

KEN: Okay...we'll get a hotel room. You and your dad can meet tomorrow at some neutral place. Talk it out then.

AMELIA: No more talk! Too much talk! Too many lies and secrets!

KEN: So what do you want to do?

AMELIA: There's a phone on the nightstand.

(*The lights dim on the Balcony.*)

Scene Seven: The Living Room

(The lights come up. Everyone is sitting, all caught within the silence. JEFFREY stirs and shifts to the edge of the couch.)

JEFFREY: Y'know, when Christine said she was leaving me, she insisted that I take Amelia. And, yes, it was for Amelia's financial welfare, but... Christine also realized that taking Amelia would help me to become a better parent...to love someone other than my work!

MAGGIE: You were younger then.

JEFFREY: *(nodding)* Yeah, and caught up in myself.

SIERRA: *(to Jeffrey)* So, what's going to happen now between you and Amelia?

JEFFREY: She's a young woman. She'll have to make her own decisions. I want to be in her life...in any way she'll allow me.

MAGGIE: *(to Quincy and Sierra)* Sorry tonight turned sour so quickly.

QUINCY: *(attempting to lighten the mood)* It *has* been an ordeal for my stomach. Maggie, I will kindly take back all my insults about your cooking if you would prepare us a take-home plate.

MAGGIE: That can be arranged.

(MAGGIE rises and taps QUINCY on the shoulder as she passes him.)

SIERRA: Jeffrey, if you wouldn't mind, I'd like to speak with Amelia.

JEFFREY: Certainly. I'll get her.

(JEFFREY rises and EXITS.)

SIERRA: *(to Jeffrey)* I'll be out on the balcony.

QUINCY: How you holding up?

SIERRA: Not bad for someone who's had to put up with you… *pero tu eres mi amorcito.

QUINCY: Mmm, *mi cielo!

(They both chuckle, as she EXITS.)

Scene Eight: The Balcony

(SIERRA waits, watching the street below. The SOUNDS of car horns and vehicle engines pepper the night. KEN ENTERS.)

SIERRA: *(jokingly)* I was expecting beauty, but got the beast instead.

KEN: *(smiling)* I can see why you and Mr. Turner married. You share a charming sense of humor.

SIERRA: Just teasing you a bit. You'll have to get
use to it to be in this family.

KEN: So I see. Cricket's on the phone. She'll be right
out. (*stepping forward*) Beautiful night.

SIERRA: Mmm. I've always enjoyed this view.

KEN: So you were close to Cricket's mom.

SIERRA: Oh, my, yes. We hit it off when Jeffrey first
introduced us. And over the years we talked
endlessly about the major jubilations…the minor
earthquakes in life.

KEN: Did you feel betrayed? Finding out about her
involvement with Simone.

SIERRA: No…and not really surprised.

KEN: Well, Cricket feels betrayed *and* surprised!

SIERRA: I can understand the surprised part. But not
betrayed. Christine was a giving mother who
would do anything for Amelia…and she did.

KEN: (*nodding*) I believe you. (*pointing to Sierra's
cane*) So, do you mind if I ask what happened?

SIERRA: Oh, this? A car accident…five years ago.

KEN: God, I'm sorry. Drunk driver?

SIERRA: Yes…my son.

(KEN tilts his head. Curious, he opens his mouth to speak, but remains silent. SIERRA notes his reaction.)

SIERRA: Q and I have a home in Stamford, Connecticut. And we keep a place here in the city so when he's in production on a play or a film, he can stay overnight. So, it was Christmas time, and Q was taking a late train home from a break on a shoot. I was leaving a party at our house to pick him up. Brandon, our son, insisted on coming with me to the station. He took the keys. I was a bit tired and didn't stop him. We were in a hurry to make it to the station...there was an unforgiving turn in the road...Brandon lost control...the car flipped once...one circular roll of metal, and all our lives were changed.

KEN: Was your son okay?

SIERRA: He survived the crash.

KEN: Thank God.

SIERRA: But I was in a coma. And after seeing my condition, he killed himself! He was twenty-one. Finishing his senior year at Dartmouth. He was planning on an MBA...going to take charge of his father's career...he had such...incredible plans.

KEN: I'm sorry. So, he blamed himself for all of it.

SIERRA: Yes. But Brandon's suicide helped Christine. Helped her to weigh the brevity of life…helped to free her from the torture of denying who she was. And I know that Christine wrote about Brandon in her journals. So, I wanted—

(*AMELIA ENTERS, her footsteps echoing.*)

KEN: Hey, Cricket.

(*AMELIA senses the mood and looks from one to the other.*)

AMELIA: What's wrong? What is it?

KEN: Just getting to know Sierra better. I'm going to give you two a little space.

(*KEN EXITS. AMELIA steps closer to SIERRA.*)

SIERRA: I was just telling Ken about Brandon.

(*AMELIA moves forward to the edge of the balcony. Looks out over the city.*)

AMELIA: Yes, it's still difficult.

SIERRA: It's getting better. (*a beat*) Well, it's been an eventful evening. All about the truth. So, let's begin with the truth about you and Ken.

AMELIA: What do you mean?

SIERRA: Well, to be blunt—he's not the person for you.

AMELIA: How can you say that? You've only known him a few hours.

SIERRA: That's all the time I needed. So, yes, you said he's faithful—as he should be! That's extremely important! But...he has a narrow mind, and a dangerous heart.

AMELIA: What are you saying?

SIERRA: Okay, how do I express this....His thinking is symptomatic of many in society, but his feelings are not empathetic to any. Perhaps, something happened to him in his childhood. But there's something more.

AMELIA: What?

SIERRA: Your lips say you love him, but there's no love in your eyes!

AMELIA: I've changed since going to college.

SIERRA: Perhaps. But you haven't lost your mind. Besides, I've only seen love in your eyes for one person.

AMELIA: *Titi*, I don't understand.

SIERRA: Yes, you do. Christine told me that she wrote about Brandon in her journals.

AMELIA: Brandon? Why would she?

SIERRA: You know why. We've been avoiding this conversation for five years.

AMELIA: My God, Brandon told you.

SIERRA: Yes.

AMELIA: You must hate me!

SIERRA: *(stepping towards Amelia)* God knows I wanted to hate you! I wanted to crush you! I wanted to shout to heaven and tear down the Jericho walls of your selfishness! I wanted to hurt you!

(SIERRA stops. Breathes deeply. AMELIA fingers her tears.)

AMELIA: But…you didn't.

SIERRA: No, I couldn't do it! As much as I wanted to, I couldn't carry that hate! You were the person my son loved. You were the mother of the grandchild I always wanted!

(AMELIA moves forward, looking into the past.)

AMELIA: The day of your party…that was the only day we could schedule at the clinic. I had my fake ID and this pounding in my head. Brandon was so sweet…so strong for me! Somehow, we got through the day. He brought me home. Then, he phoned me from your party. He wanted to come back and see me. I told him not to. I just

needed to shut the world out. But not him! I
never wanted to shut him out! He was hurting...
and he said he was going to drown himself...no,
he said lose himself in an ocean of liquor and
regret.

SIERRA: I saw him hang up the phone, take a bottle
of whiskey into his room. When he didn't come
back out, I followed him inside...he told me
everything. Told me he loved you! Told me he
wanted the child.

AMELIA: (*sobbing*) I was so scared!

SIERRA: You were seventeen, Amelia! We've both
lost. We've both felt pain. Brandon gone.
A baby gone. Your mother gone. (*moves closer
to Amelia*) And now, your father? Simone? Have
you lost them, too? Are you going to give them
up?

AMELIA: (*struggling for words*) I can't loosen this
tightness...here inside. Nothing seems right.
Nothing's balanced. Everything is twisted and
turned on its side.

SIERRA: Life often wrenches...hurts! That's why you
have to hold tightly to those who help you to
find the calm. That's what Christine called it
when she played her cello. With the poetry she
could shout her voice...with the cello she found
the calm.

(*AMELIA turns to face SIERRA, wiping the tears
away.*)

AMELIA: I'm so sorry about Brandon.

SIERRA: I know. And I knew I had to forgive you to
find a calm space here inside. Now, you need
to forgive yourself for your teenage decisions.
For Brandon's death. Then, forgive your father
and mother... forgive Simone. What you did at
seventeen was out of confusion. What they did
was out of love.

(*SIERRA reaches out her hand. AMELIA steps
to her, taking SIERRA's hand.*)

AMELIA: I was in love with Brandon!

SIERRA: And he was in love with you!

(*The lights go down on the Balcony.*)

Scene Nine: The Living Room

(*The lights rise quickly in the Living Room. MAGGIE
ENTERS from the Kitchen, carrying a casserole dish
covered with aluminum foil.*)

MAGGIE: This should help.

(*QUINCY takes the dish and smells longingly.*)

QUINCY: Mm, Pasta Primavera!

MAGGIE: Make certain Sierra gets some.

QUINCY: I'll make certain she gets what's coming to
      her.

JEFFREY: Wait, let me get Amelia.

QUINCY: No, don't trouble her. Just tell her that my
      wedding present to her and Ken will be a set of
      white sheets. I'll just need to know what size
      Ken wears.

JEFFREY: (*to Maggie*) What's he talking about?

MAGGIE: I'll explain later.

      (*SIERRA and AMELIA ENTER from the
      Balcony.*)

SIERRA: So, I see we're leaving.

QUINCY: And with our share of the goodies.

SIERRA: Knowing you, my share will somehow
      become your share.

QUINCY: A prophet in our midst. And such a
      beautiful one!

      (*AMELIA takes a step towards the bedroom.*)

AMELIA: (*calling*) Ken!

      (*QUINCY opens his free arm to AMELIA. She
      moves in for a hug as KEN ENTERS from the
      bedroom.*)

AMELIA: Good-bye, Uncle Q.

QUINCY: Good to see you again, my dear.

KEN: A pleasure to meet you, Mr. Turner. It's been…
provocative.

QUINCY: Ken, sometimes inebriation and
provocation can lead to revelation. You're a
work in progress, but there's great promise for
you.

KEN: I think there's a compliment somewhere in there.

QUINCY: (*to Jeffrey and Maggie*) Until tomorrow
night at the theater, my friends. Ciao!

SIERRA: Good night.

KEN: Oh, Mr. Turner, wait! One more thing…who's
Sugihara?

QUINCY: (*to Sierra*) One more story?

SIERRA: As if I could stop you.

QUINCY: Well, a few years ago, Jeffrey and I were
involved with a business deal with some
Japanese investors that fell apart. We both lost a
great deal of money. Jeffrey, in a sort of Old
Testament fashion, wanted to rain down his
Sodom and Gomorrah fire and destruction on all
Japanese.

JEFFREY: I was beyond anger! We lost over—

(QUINCY lifts a hand to interrupt Jeffrey.)

QUINCY: So, similar to Abraham in the elliptical book of Genesis, I argued that I could find at least one Japanese person that even Jeffrey would call good. *(looking at Jeffrey)* Maybe Jeffrey wouldn't mind telling you the rest.

JEFFREY: Oh, I don't need this tonight!

> *(QUINCY shifts his body weight and gives a demanding stare. Now, everyone is staring at Jeffrey.)*

Okay, okay! *(to Ken)* Sugihara was a Japanese diplomat to Lithuania during World War Two. He and his wife…well, they disobeyed orders from the Japanese government and signed exit visas for Jewish refugees from Poland who were hiding in Lithuania…with the visas, the Jews were able to escape the Nazis…some to Russia…some as far as the Caribbean… Sugihara saved thousands of Jews.

KEN: *(thoughtfully)* Never heard of him before.

QUINCY: And now that you have? *(extending his hand)* Take care of yourself, Ken.

> *(The two shake hands. Then, QUINCY and SIERRA ad-lib their goodbyes as THEY EXIT.)*

MAGGIE: Amelia, can I get you something?

AMELIA: No. Actually, we'll be taking the eleven
o'clock train tonight back to Ithaca.

JEFFREY: You're leaving tonight?

KEN: Yes, we've decided it's best.

AMELIA: As soon as we gather our things.

MAGGIE: (*angrily*) Amelia, you can't do that! You
can't just leave now!

AMELIA: (*sarcastically*) Sorry to destroy your dinner.

MAGGIE: It's not about dinner, and you know it!
What more does your father have to do! You
can't give him one night!

AMELIA: Listen, this doesn't concern you!

MAGGIE: Of course it does! It's not just about you
and your whining self pity! Yes, there were
things kept from you! Yes, you were hurt! But
hurting your father won't change one moment of
the past. You ungrateful little witch!

AMELIA: Witch? I expected *bitch* from you.

MAGGIE: And I expected a young woman, not some
petulant child! You don't know about the hell
you escaped by having a father who loves you!
To be able to have a family that cares! You
didn't spend your whole childhood fighting to
survive! What have you ever had to fight for,
Amelia?

AMELIA: Don't lecture me!

MAGGIE: And don't insult me or your father any
longer! (*rushing over and opening the door*)
You want to leave? Go for it, Cricket!

AMELIA: (*to Jeffrey*) Well, maybe you ought to keep
this one. At least she has brains enough to string
together a sentence!

JEFFREY: Enough! Dammit! Don't you ever speak
about Maggie like that again!

AMELIA: (*tearfully*) It's all been said then!

> (*AMELIA backs away slowly and then EXITS
> for the Guest Bedroom. KEN nods silently and
> goes after her. MAGGIE slips her arm around
> JEFFREY's waist as the lights go down.*)

Scene Ten: Penn Station

(*AMELIA and KEN ENTER from stage left. The
background NOISES in the train station are as active as
in the earlier scene. AMELIA and KEN cross to the
vacant bench. KEN checks his watch as AMELIA sits,
placing her overnight bag on the floor.*)

KEN: Damn, your suitcase is heavier.

AMELIA: My mom's journals are inside.

KEN: Oh, okay. We should get the boarding call in a few minutes. Something to drink?

(AMELIA shakes her head.)

I'm hungry! I'm tired! What a rotten night! You must feel terrible, too!

AMELIA: Yes, I'm drained.

(KEN sits beside her. Takes her hand.)

KEN: We'll survive this.

(She leans her head on his shoulder.)

KEN: Well, that Quincy Turner was an experience. In his movies, he's so dignified. But, he had a bug up his ass tonight.

AMELIA: He's been a great friend to my father. He and Sierra are family.

KEN: In this case, you mean *like* family, right? No more secrets and surprises. Quincy isn't really going to turn out to be your father's lost brother, is he? I mean, there's a black sheep in the family, and then there's a *black* sheep!

AMELIA: No more to reveal. At least, not tonight.

KEN: Good.

AMELIA: But I have to be honest...I'm going to miss

Aunt— I'm going to miss Simone. I could talk to
her about anything.

KEN: Obviously, she didn't reciprocate. Besides,
the last thing we'll need is her hanging around
when the baby comes. Did you tell her?

AMELIA: Yes, tonight when she arrived.

KEN: Damn…well, if it's a girl, we won't be naming her
Simone.

AMELIA: No, I guess not.

KEN: Now, we can work on other decisions.

AMELIA: What other decisions?

KEN: Since you're my fiance, maybe we can work it
out with my insurance company to cover you.

(AMELIA sits up.)

AMELIA: What's wrong with my doctor? I've been
with her for years.

KEN: Well, she's fine for the pregnancy. But I don't
know if she's qualified to run the tests we'll
need.

AMELIA: Tests? What are you talking about?

KEN: Well, I think that it would be wise to check
out some things. They can do that now. It was in
a recent study from Johns-Hopkins. Researchers

were conducting gene studies and stumbled onto
the Z chromosome factor, or some such thing.

AMELIA: I'm not following you.

(He turns to her. Holds both her hands.)

KEN: Well, from what I understand, doctors can do a
series of tests...whether or not the tests could
indicate anything this early in your pregnancy, I
don't know.

AMELIA: (*frustrated*) Ken, will you say what you
have to say!

KEN: Supposedly, there's a chromosome test that
can determine whether the baby will be born
with...abnormalities. Can tell if the baby will
be...normal.

AMELIA: Normal?

KEN: You know...deformities. Down's syndrome,
spina bifida, the gay thing.

AMELIA: (*understanding*) Oh, my God!

KEN: We have to think about our child! It's hard
enough in this world without—

AMELIA: (*interrupting*) Without what? And if the
tests tell you what you don't want to hear?

KEN: Then, we take the necessary steps.

AMELIA: Necessary steps? (*standing angrily*)
You're serious, aren't you? You and all your
talk about Pro-Life!

(*AMELIA takes a few steps away.*)

KEN: I am Pro-Life, but I'm thinking about the
child. I know we feel the same about this!

AMELIA: No, *we* don't! How can you so coldly
calculate about our child?

KEN: It's not just about the baby! It's also about us!
The kind of family we want and don't want!

AMELIA: What about being happy with a healthy
baby...being the best parents we can!

KEN: Of course! That's what I'm talking about...
having a healthy kid!

AMELIA: (*sternly*) My mother was not abnormal, Ken!
Simone is not deformed!

(*KEN steps to her.*)

KEN: Hey, you're making it sound evil! This is not
the place for us to discuss this!

AMELIA: Why not here, Ken? If *you* don't care about
your child, why should anyone else care!

KEN: You're getting upset!

AMELIA: Upset—you think? Tonight, my life has been shattered into these bizarre pieces! And somewhere beneath all the rubble I'm supposed to understand my mom's love! (*a beat*) God, I wish you had met her...she was so patient...had an infectious laugh! And her poetry... beautiful!

KEN: What are you talking about, Amelia?

AMELIA: I'm talking about Mom...her writing and music. And I feel guilty because maybe I'm the reason she held herself back. So, now you tell me we have to reject our child if tests find a lurking chromosome!

KEN: We're jumping ahead of ourselves here. I'm just saying that we don't have to have any surprises.

AMELIA: Ken, we should be exploding with joy because we're able to have a baby! (*sadly*) Some fathers never get that chance! To have and to know his own child! (*a beat*) Simone was right! Mom should have...(*loudly*) have yelled out the truth so that everyone would stop and hear!

KEN: Cricket, you acting strange. You're talking about one thing and then another!

AMELIA: (*loudly*) I'm Amelia Rosewall, the daughter of Christine Rosewall!

KEN: Amelia!

AMELIA: (*shouting*) Christine Rosewall was a mother!

A poet! A musician!

KEN: (*looking around*) Quiet down!

AMELIA: (*shouting louder*) And, yes, Christine
Rosewall, my mother, was a—

KEN: (*interrupting loudly*) —No, Amelia, stop!
Don't say it!

AMELIA: (*calmly*) Why, not? Why can't I shout it
out?

KEN: *(standing)* Because there are just some things
you don't say out loud! You're making us look
ridiculous!

AMELIA: Who cares what these strangers think?

KEN: I care! Now, will you please sit down!

> *(KEN offers his hand, but AMELIA sits down on
> her own.)*

> Like I said, this is not the place to hold this
> discussion!

AMELIA: Maybe there's an available closet.

> *(KEN snickers angrily and shakes his head.
> He straightens his clothes and sits on the bench.
> AMELIA looks off into her thoughts.)*

ANNOUNCER'S VOICE: First call for the eleven

o'clock train to points north, including
Poughkeepsie, Ithaca, Buffalo, and Lynchburg!

KEN: That's us! We better go!

*(AMELIA moves reluctantly. She lifts the
overnight bag as KEN grabs the suitcases. She
follows him as they move stage right. She stops
abruptly.)*

AMELIA: Wait!

KEN: What?

AMELIA: I need to get into my suitcase.

*(KEN groans impatiently. He lowers the
luggage. AMELIA unzips her suitcase and
removes her mother's journals, stacking them on
the floor. Then, she closes the suitcase.)*

KEN: Amelia, what are you doing? You can throw those
away later!

*(AMELIA opens her overnight bag and places
the journals inside. She stands and faces him.)*

AMELIA: You're right. There're some things we need to
discuss. There's one more secret from my past
that I need to tell you. But not tonight! So, go
back to Ithaca. I'm going to stay in the city for a
day or so.

KEN: I don't believe this! This is crazy! What is it that
you want?

AMELIA: Take the luggage and go back to Ithaca.

KEN: (*throwing up his hands*) This has been the
strangest night of my life! You know you're
ruining my Spring Break!

AMELIA: I'm sorry, Ken. But, right now, there's
something more important!

KEN: And what the hell does that mean?

AMELIA: It means I'll call you.

KEN: You'll call me? I'm supposed to go back to
Ithaca and spend the week alone!

AMELIA: Then, go to California.

KEN: Oh, right! Go home and tell my family all
that's happened tonight!

AMELIA: Yes, you should shout it out!

KEN: (*enraged*) Let me shout this out, Amelia! *(loudly)*
You can go to hell! You and your whole nutty,
fruitcake family!

*(KEN kicks her suitcase and storms off stage
right. AMELIA pulls the suitcase over to the
bench. She fingers her overnight bag and
removes her StarTAC Flip Phone. She slowly
pushes numbers.)*

AMELIA: *(into phone)* Hello…Aunt Simone…yes, it's me. I want to come over…maybe we can talk while you pack for your trip…yes, it's me.

(The lights go down.)

Scene Eleven

(In his Townhouse, Jeffrey stands at the end table by the couch. He wears a bathrobe over his shirt and slacks. He lifts the phone and punches the numbers.

At downstage left, in Quincy's Home Office, a chair is next to a small table that holds a phone. The phone rings, and Quincy ENTERS. He, too, wears a bathrobe over his shirt and slacks.)

QUINCY: *(into phone)* Hello.

JEFFREY: Q, it's me. Didn't wake you and Sierra, did I?

QUINCY: Naw, after the first sip of amaretto, she was asleep. I'm just finishing off Maggie's casserole that I hid from her.

JEFFREY: Smart man. Listen…I need to tell you something.

QUINCY: *(sitting)* Okay, what's on your mind?

JEFFREY: *(pacing)* I mentioned that Simone and I

had an explosive confrontation at Christine's
funeral. That wasn't the first time I deliberately
went after her. I just didn't know how to deal
with it all!

QUINCY: What do you mean?

JEFFREY: The fact that Christine was cheating on
me...with a woman. I lost it, Q! I was helpless
and humiliated at the same time! So I tried to
validate my manhood with every woman I met! I
just needed to prove that I was man enough to
please a woman! I know it probably sounds
crazy. But, I didn't know what to think! I hated
Simone for years! I wanted to physically hurt
her! I finally had to talk to a therapist. And
between sessions, I was sucking down bottles of
scotch for breakfast!

QUINCY: But it wasn't about *you*, Jeff! Christine
needed to be herself!

JEFFREY: Yeah, it took me a while to figure that out.
Y'know, you said something to me at the time
that really helped.

QUINCY: I did?

JEFFREY: You told me..."Jeff, you're not the first
husband to be cheated on...you're not the first
father to fear raising a child. But *you* are the
only man who can get yourself through both
situations."

QUINCY: I said all that?

JEFFREY: And more. I realized that being a husband isn't just about sexual satisfaction. And being a father is more than just making a baby.

QUINCY: Well, I'm glad I could help.

JEFFREY: Would've helped me more if you'd told me earlier. For a year, I was seeing a Manhattan shrink at three-hundred bucks an hour!

QUINCY: And Amelia? You need to give her a call, too.

JEFFREY: I should, but I don't even know where she is right now. And if she's not at her place, I can't tell her what I'm feeling in a two-minute message on an answering machine!

QUINCY: A life can be changed in two minutes...and love can be expressed in even less.

JEFFREY: Okay, okay...thanks, my friend.

QUINCY: Good night.

> *(The light over Quincy fades. Jeffrey pushes the buttons on the phone, and waits.)*

JEFFREY: *(into phone)* Amelia...it's your father. I'm so sorry we didn't have more time to talk. I know you still have questions. But I want you to know this...I would give away all that I have, if you and I could be together as a family. I know it won't be easy, and there'll be some more tears... but *you* are the jewel that makes me a

rich man. Let's find the value in what we have
now, and not linger on the things from the past
that we can't change. Call me...and I'll be here
for you. Love you...dad.

(The light dims over Jeffrey as he ends the call.)

Scene Twelve

*(A spotlight opens downstage center. AMELIA ENTERS
holding Christine's green-covered journal. She reads
from the page, but closes the book. Recites from heart.)*

AMELIA: when the spotlight passes by,
    no friendly touch upon my face,
    I once again move in darkness,
    I once more grab the edges
    of my difference in this dim lit space,
    filled with mornings of solitary yearnings,
    and evenings where there's dark despair,
    forever my passions simmering and burning,
    forever striving, rising in mid-air

    in a place that I call home,
    away from the gazes, the scowls
    of those who think they know
    who I am, those who are prone
    to lead me along steps they sow,
    into circles they fear to walk alone.

    how can I break from their grasp?
    that pulling, clutching, drowning of my soul?
    if it were an easy task, I would deny myself,

embrace their likeness as a way to become
whole.

I stood in the shadow of regrets,
showered in my isolated tears,
baptized with longings and secrets,
hiding from whispers and vicious sneers,

but this melancholy has reached an end,
a new world begins where I care not
if you praise me or condescend.
pass me by if you choose,
label me with epithets and spiteful names,
I refuse to deny, to further self-abuse
to win your favor, your unfulfilling fame,
from this harbor, inside, I find my cornerstone,
to sculpt, to sing my life in infinite overtones,
my dreams and spirit a burning legacy,
an affirming shout—I'm me! I'm me!

(The lights fade to black. The curtain falls.)

THE END

*GLOSSARY/ SPANISH

¡Ay Bendito! – Oh, my Lord!

¡Dios mio! – My God!

¡Mi cariño! – Hello, darling!

mi cielo – you are my world

¡Mi corazón! – my heart!

¡Mi querida amiga! – my dear friend!

pero tu eres mi amorcito – but you are my sweetheart

¿Que?¡Eso es una cosa terrible de decir! – What? That's a terrible thing to say!

Titi – Auntie

ACKNOWLEDGMENTS

This play has maintained a front row position in my mind for years, but for various reasons, I would return-and-leave to develop other projects. Finally, in November 2016, I had a dramatic reading of the play at the Road Company Theater in North Hollywood, California. The responses from those attending were encouraging and positive, and I moved forward to revise and develop the play to be performed in September 2017.

Shout allowed me to examine the various issues and themes that continue to serve as a foundation to my writing, and either briefly or at length, I have met all seven characters in this play during my adult life. As they intersect, they all have their strengths and weaknesses that I've observed in most people, including myself. And I've come to understand that most people are confronting and/or living with the twin siblings of joy-and-sorrow in their lives. Some keep the twins hidden deep inside, while others have to release them out loud to survive the extremities of spiraling elations and unbearable sadness. Writing about these mad twins has given me a way to cope with their prevalence.

I owe my gratitude to several people who helped me to transform the play into a final book form: my wife, Beverly A. Tate, and my friends, Juan Carlos Parrilla and Vique Mora. To my friend, Ben Guillory, I'm very grateful for his comments and thoughts that grace the rear cover. And, once again, I am indebted to the creativity and talents of my artistic friend, Brandon Clark, who designed the cover.